Ted & Me

Sometimes you can change history.
And sometimes history can change you.

Also by Dan Gutman

The Get Rich Quick Club
Johnny Hangtime
Casey Back at Bat

Baseball Card Adventures:

Honus & Me
Jackie & Me
Babe & Me
Shoeless Joe & Me

Mickey & Me
Abner & Me
Satch & Me
Jim & Me

Ray & Me
Roberto & Me

The Genius Files:

Mission Unstoppable
Never Say Genius

My Weirder School:

Miss Child Has Gone Wild!
Mr. Harrison Is Embarrassin'!
Mrs. Lilly Is Silly!
Mr. Burke Is Berserk!

My Weird School Daze:

Mrs. Dole Is Out of Control!
Mr. Sunny Is Funny!
Mr. Granite Is from Another Planet!
Coach Hyatt Is a Riot!
Officer Spence Makes No Sense!
Mrs. Jafee Is Daffy!

Dr. Brad Has Gone Mad!
Miss Laney Is Zany!
Mrs. Lizzy Is Dizzy!
Miss Mary Is Scary!
Mr. Tony Is Full of Baloney!
Miss Leakey Is Freaky!

My Weird School:

Miss Daisy Is Crazy!
Mr. Klutz Is Nuts!
Mrs. Roopy Is Loopy!
Ms. Hannah Is Bananas!
Miss Small Is off the Wall!
Mr. Hynde Is Out of His Mind!
Mrs. Cooney Is Loony!
Ms. LaGrange Is Strange!
Miss Lazar Is Bizarre!
Mr. Docker Is off His Rocker!

Mrs. Kormel Is Not Normal!
Ms. Todd Is Odd!
Mrs. Patty Is Batty!
Miss Holly Is Too Jolly!
Mr. Macky Is Wacky!
Ms. Coco Is Loco!
Miss Suki Is Kooky!
Mrs. Yonkers Is Bonkers!
Dr. Carbles Is Losing His Marbles!
Mr. Louie Is Screwy!

Ms. Krup Cracks Me Up!

Ted & Me

A Baseball Card Adventure

Dan Gutman

HARPER
An Imprint of HarperCollinsPublishers

Library of Congress Cataloging-in-Publication Data
Gutman, Dan.
    Ted & me : a baseball card adventure / Dan Gutman.—1st ed.
      p.   cm.
    Summary: When Stosh travels back in time to 1941 in hopes of prevent-
ing the Japanese attack on Pearl Harbor that brought the United States into
World War II, he meets Ted Williams, one of the greatest hitters in baseball
history. Includes notes about Williams' life and career.
    ISBN 978-0-06-123487-3 (trade bdg.)
    ISBN 978-0-06-123488-0 (lib. bdg.)
    [1. Time travel—Fiction. 2. Baseball—Fiction. 3. Williams, Ted,
1918–2002—Fiction. 4. Conduct of life—Fiction. 5. Pearl Harbor (Hawaii),
Attack on, 1941—Fiction. 6. World War, 1939–1945—Fiction.] I. Title. II.
Title: Ted and me.
PZ7.G9846Ted 2012   2011019359
[Fic]—dc23   CIP
                                             AC

Typography by Cara Petrus
12 13 14 15 16   LP/RRDH   10 9 8 7 6 5 4 3 2
❖
First Edition

To Ray Dimetrosky, Howard Wolf,
and Craig Provorny

Acknowledgments

THANKS TO COXEY TOOGOOD OF THE INDEPENDENCE National Historical Park, Dave Kelly of the Library of Congress, JoAnn Pure of the Haddonfield Public Library, Steve Barr of Little League International, Pat Kelly of the National Baseball Hall of Fame, Zach Rice, Nina Wallace, Alan Kors, Peter Blau, and Ed Maugher.

His weakness was his anger, and his anger was his strength.

—Leigh Montville, in
Ted Williams: The Biography of an American Hero

Note to Readers

TED WILLIAMS WAS KNOWN FOR USING "SALTY" LANGUAGE. I wanted to bring him to life, but I didn't want to put curse words in this book. When you see the occasional "!@#$%!," that's Ted cursing. If you're reading this book aloud, I suggest you replace "!@#$%!" with "bleep" or "bleeping."

Please, no angry letters.

Introduction

WITH A BASEBALL CARD IN MY HAND, I AM THE MOST POW-
erful person in the world. With a card in my hand, I
can do something the president of the United States
can't do, the most intelligent genius on the planet
can't do, the best athlete in the universe can't do.

I can travel through time.

—Joe Stoshack

1

It Ain't Over 'Til It's Over

"YOU READY, STOSH?" MY COACH, FLIP VALENTINI, ASKED me.

"Ready as I'll ever be."

I never thought in a million years that I would get the chance to play in the Little League World Series. Some kids dream of playing in the majors or the Super Bowl, or taking that last shot to beat the buzzer in the NBA Finals. Not me. None of those things ever crossed my mind. I figure only the best of the best get *that* far.

I mean, I'm a pretty decent ballplayer, don't get me wrong. I can hit, field, throw, and run better than most kids. But let's be realistic. I'm not even the best in the 13-year-old age group. There are kids who are way better than I am, much stronger and bigger than me. I can't compete with them. Those are the kids who'll make it to the top, I figure, if they're lucky and don't get hurt along the way. All I ever hoped to do was play in the Little League World Series.

And here I was.

Williamsport, Pennsylvania. Every August, the best Little League teams gather here to see which one is the best of all. And it's truly a *world* series. It's not like in Major League Baseball, where the "world" consists of a bunch of American teams and the Toronto Blue Jays. In the Little League World Series, there are kids from Taiwan, the Dominican Republic, Japan, South America—all over.

It had been a long road. First I was picked to play shortstop for the all-star team in my town—Louisville, Kentucky. We have this one lefty pitcher, Kyle, who can throw over 80 miles an hour consistently. I've had to hit against him when we played his team, the Exterminators; and he is just about untouchable. We nicknamed him the Mutant Man because he's six feet tall and his arms are just about that long too.

Anyway, with Kyle on the mound, we swept through the district, sectional, and regional tournaments. That got us into the World Series, where we had to compete against fifteen other teams. Kyle threw a couple of no-hitters; and the next thing we knew, we were facing the Dominican Republic in the Little League World Series Championship game. For me, it was a dream come true.

WELCOME TO VOLUNTEER STADIUM the sign said as our bus pulled into the parking lot. When we walked through the gate, all these people were clapping and cheering.

"Is somebody famous here?" I asked, craning my neck to look around and spot some celebrity.

"Yeah," said our catcher, Cubby Abrams, *"us."*

I don't think I ever saw that many people in one place at one time. Cubby said he heard that the stadium could hold 45,000 spectators. Back home we had some games with ten parents watching us play, and most of them would just sit there talking on their cell phones or texting the whole time. I started to feel that nervous feeling in the pit of my stomach.

Out past the outfield fences I could see lots of people sitting on the lawn. Some of them were holding banners: GO, LOUISVILLE! and USA! There were signs in Spanish too.

My mom was in the stands, down the third-base line somewhere. She had driven over ten hours to Williamsport with my aunt Liz and cousin Samantha. My dad is wheelchair-bound, and he couldn't make the trip; but he would be watching on TV. It was okay. My folks split up a few years ago, and it's better for everybody when they're not together. They just start arguing.

While we warmed up, people were pointing cameras at us and asking us to sign autographs. We were drinking it all in. ESPN was there. They had these robotic TV cameras on wires that were swooping all around to film us. Millions of people were going to be watching the game. The Goodyear blimp was

3

floating overhead.

"We are superstars, dude!" our third baseman, Tyler Harvey, said to me.

Coach Valentini told us not to look over at the Dominican players as they warmed up on the first-base side, but I couldn't resist peeking at them. Some of those guys were *huge*. It was hard to believe they were all younger than 14. But then, some of our guys were pretty big too. Like Kyle.

Flip Valentini is really old, and we had to help him into the dugout so he could give us his usual pregame pep talk. If Flip fell down and broke his hip or something, it would be horrible.

The previous night at the Econo Lodge where we were staying, Flip called me into his room after dinner. He told me this would probably be his last season coaching. He said his arthritis is getting worse, and he is finding it harder and harder to get around. He put his arm on my shoulder and told me I was sort of like a son to him. I told him he was sort of like a dad to me. We didn't cry or anything, but it was pretty intense. And then Flip said something that took me by surprise.

"Stosh, when they play the national anthem before the game tomorrow," he said, "how 'bout you carry the flag out there?"

I didn't know what to say. To be honest, I didn't want to do it. I mean, it's a big honor and all, but I didn't deserve it. I'm not the best player on our team. And besides, I didn't want everyone staring at me. It would be embarrassing. What if I tripped and fell or something and the flag hit the ground? Of course, I didn't want to let Flip down either.

"Do I have to?" I asked hesitantly.

"Fuhgetaboutit, Stosh," he replied. "Kyle can do it."

But I could see the disappointment in his eyes as I left the room.

Now the whole team was huddled around Flip in the dugout. He reminded us that the last time Louisville made it to the World Series was 2002. A long time ago. They'd won it that year too. Now it was our turn.

"Y'know how many kids play Little League ball?" Flip asked us.

"How many?" asked our leftfielder, Josh Cresswell.

"How should I know?" Flip said. "Zillions. Fuhgetaboutit. A lot. Point is, those kids ain't here today. *You* are. Win or lose, you're gonna remember this day for the rest of your lives. So don't screw up. 'Cause if you make some bonehead play, they're gonna show it on TV tonight."

Flip isn't so great at pep talks. He went on for a while. Some of it was inspirational. Sometimes we had to cover our mouths with our gloves so Flip wouldn't see us giggling. But Flip is Flip, and we love him.

We ran out onto the field and lined up along the first-base line. The Dominican team lined up on the third-base line. When Kyle came out carrying the American flag, I felt a little bad. That could have been me. I didn't look at Flip.

A marching band played the national anthem. A veteran of the Iraq War came on the field to throw out the first pitch. He only had one leg, but he threw a strike, anyway. Everybody gave him a standing ovation.

We were the home team, so we ran out to our positions for the first inning. While Kyle warmed up, I took a minute to look around. It was a beautiful field. The infield was perfectly groomed. It wasn't like the crummy fields we've played on back home. I smoothed the dirt around my shortstop position, anyway. There wasn't a pebble to be found. I wouldn't have to worry about a grounder taking a bad hop and hitting me in the face.

It didn't matter. I didn't field a ball in the first inning. Kyle just mowed them down. Nine pitches, nine strikes. He was on fire. The Dominican kids looked like a bunch of chumps.

We were feeling pretty good until we got a look at *their* pitcher: Jose. He wasn't a big guy, and he didn't throw all that hard. But he had this weird, deceptive motion. Sometimes he released the ball overhand, and on the next pitch he'd cross you up and throw it sidearm. He threw each pitch at a different speed, and he had pinpoint control. It was hard to pick up the ball. We went down one, two, three. I didn't get the chance to hit in the first inning because Flip put me eighth in the batting order.

I finally got a chance to hit in the third inning. Jose started me off with a straight fastball right over the plate, which I swung over for strike one. I took a hack at the next one too, but it was a little outside and I missed it. I tried to think of everything Flip had taught me about hitting with two strikes. *Guard the plate. Choke up a little. Just make contact.*

None of it mattered. Jose blew a fastball by me, and I almost fell down swinging at it. I didn't feel that bad. Nobody else on our team was hitting the kid either.

It was shaping up to be a real pitcher's duel. Kyle would go out and make the Dominicans look silly, and then Jose would do the same to us. We managed one dinky hit through six innings, and Kyle was still working on a no-hitter in the seventh.

He walked the first batter, which is always dangerous. The next guy bunted him over to second. One out. Runner in scoring position. I edged a little over toward the second-base bag to keep the runner honest.

Kyle was rattled and threw the next pitch in the dirt. When the ball got away from Cubby Abrams, the runner dashed to third. This was getting serious now.

Kyle looked determined, and he struck out the next guy on three pitches. Two outs. We were looking good, but there was that runner on third. One little mistake on our part and he would score. And in a game like this, one run could be enough to win it.

Their next batter was a lefty, so I shifted over a few feet closer to second base. This kid had already struck out twice, so I wasn't too worried about him.

"No batter," I hollered. "You got this guy, Kyle."

Kyle threw a strike and a ball, and on the next pitch the batter took a swing and sent a grounder skittering up the middle. Kyle stabbed his glove at the ball as it went by, but he couldn't reach it.

I reacted instinctively, running to my left. When the ball skipped off the pitcher's mound, it changed the trajectory just a little bit, as I knew it would. I also knew it was going to be a tough play.

"Dive, Stosh!" somebody yelled.

Nobody had to tell me that. If I could just stop the ball and knock it down, I could pick it up and throw the guy out at first. That would be the third out, and the run wouldn't score. I had made this play plenty of times.

But I didn't make it this time. I dove, stretched my arm as far as I could; but the ball ticked off the end of my glove and rolled into the outfield. The runner from third scored, and we were behind, 1–0. The official scorer didn't give me an error. The play was ruled a hit.

I kicked the dirt. One more inch and I would've had it. *One more inch.* Flip always tells us that baseball is a game of inches.

After Kyle got the third out, everybody in the dugout was trying to make me feel better, telling me to forget about it.

"Nice try, Stosh," Flip said. "Good effort."

But I knew that I could have reached that ball. If only I had a better jump on it. If only I had a bigger glove. If only I was an inch taller. Flip always tells us that if you can touch the ball, you should be able to catch it.

We went into the ninth inning still trailing, 1–0. I looked at the lineup card on the wall of the dugout. I was due to bat fourth. So if nobody got on base, I wouldn't get another chance to hit. And if one of our guys *did* get on base, I could be in position to drive in the run and tie the game . . . or make the final out.

Part of me wanted to get the chance to be the hero. Part of me, I must admit, hoped we'd go down one, two, three so I wouldn't be our last batter with the game on the line.

Jose *must* be getting tired, I figured. He had thrown over a hundred pitches. Somebody was warming up in the Dominican bull pen. They could replace Jose at any moment.

Raul Perez, our second baseman, led off. He launched a high fly ball to leftfield. We were all holding our breath in the dugout, but the ball was caught a few feet in front of the fence. One out.

Tyler Harvey was up. He got the ball up in the air too, but just to the infield. The third baseman grabbed it. Two outs.

We were down to our last out. Cubby Abrams was up. I walked out to the on-deck circle.

"Save my ups, man!" I shouted to Cubby as he stepped up to the plate.

It was a lie. I didn't want Cubby to save my ups. I wanted him to make the last out so I wouldn't have to. I don't like to admit it, but it's true. Nobody wants to make the final out.

Cubby took a ball and a strike; and then as the next pitch was coming in, he did something that blew everyone's mind—he squared around to bunt!

The third baseman was playing way back, guarding the line to prevent an extra-base hit. He had no chance to pick up the ball as it rolled a few inches from the foul line. The pitcher was too far away to get it. Cubby wasn't a fast runner, but he was digging for first. The catcher tore off his mask and pounced on the ball. He made a great play getting the ball to first just as Cubby was crossing the bag.

"Safe!" yelled the umpire.

Oh, no. We had a runner at first. That meant Cubby represented the tying run, and I represented the winning run . . . or the last out. Everybody on our bench was going crazy.

"Go get 'em, Stosh!"

"Stosh, you can do it, man!"

Why does this always happen to *me*? I looked around the stands trying to find my mom, but I couldn't see her. She was probably hiding her face. If it wasn't me up there, I wouldn't want to watch either.

Before I could walk up to the plate, Flip climbed

slowly out of the dugout and put his arm around me. It was just reassurance. There was nothing he could teach me at this point that he hadn't already drilled into me a hundred times before.

"Okeydokey, Stosh," he said quietly. "Relax. Hold yer bat nice and loose. If the first one looks good, take a rip at it. Whale on that baby. Nice level swing. Just like I taughtcha. Now go get 'im.'"

I picked up my bat, a 32-ounce Louisville Slugger. I used to swing a lighter bat, but Flip told us the heavier the bat, the harder you can hit the ball. I always follow Flip's advice. He picked out this bat especially for me.

I glanced down the foul lines as I walked up to the plate. Two hundred and twenty-five feet. I had hit a ball that far once or twice. It would be cool to slam a walk-off homer. That would be the high point of my life.

But right now I just wanted to get a single. Advance the runner. Even a walk would be okay. Let somebody *else* be the hero.

Jose looked at me. He certainly knew what I had done so far in the game: a strikeout in the third inning, a pop-up in the sixth. His first pitch—overhand—missed outside. I looked at our dugout to see if Flip was going to give me a sign, but he was just clapping his hands and shouting encouragement.

I decided to take the next pitch and hope for ball two, but Jose grooved it—sidearm—over the inside corner. One and one.

Okay, he wasn't going to walk me. And I sure wasn't going to go down looking. He knew that. Jose threw his change-up—overhand again—and I was way ahead of it. Strike two.

I was down to my last strike. *We* were down to our last strike. Everybody on the bench was yelling and screaming. People in the stands had rally towels over their heads because they couldn't bring themselves to watch. I took a deep breath. So did Jose.

Protect the plate, I told myself. *And relax. But be aggressive.* It was all a head game now, between Jose and me. Would he come in over the top with a hard one? Or sidearm it in slowly? High or low? Inside or outside corner? Would he waste one off the plate, hoping I'd go fishing for it?

Stop thinking so much, I yelled at myself. *Just see the ball and hit the ball.*

Jose went into his windup, and this time he was throwing *underhand.* It took me a millisecond to process that information and make the slight adjustment. I would have liked to let the pitch go by. But it was looking like a strike, so I had to swing.

Late. Air. Nothing.

Strike three. End of game. Final score: 1–0.

The Dominican kids jumped all over each other. Every camera was pointed at them celebrating, not at us looking depressed. I dragged my Louisville Slugger back to the dugout. A few of the guys were crying.

It was all over so fast. I felt that I had snapped my

fingers in the first inning, and now it was the ninth inning.

There would be no walk-off home run. No come-from-behind heroics. No miracle finish.

My dad once told me that Yogi Berra said, "It ain't over 'til it's over."

Well, it was over. We lost, and that was that.

2

A Mission

It took a few days for life to return to normal after we got back from Williamsport. Me and the guys weren't celebrities anymore. We had to go back to cleaning our rooms, mowing our lawns, doing our summer reading—boring stuff like that.

I was playing Nintendo in the living room a couple of days after we got home. My mom was paying the bills in the den. She was all worried because she'd read an article in a magazine that said it costs over $100,000 to send a kid to college for four years, and she doesn't have anywhere *near* that kind of money.

"I don't have to go to college," I told her. "I'll get a good job."

"You're going to college," she insisted. "That's how you'll *get* a good job."

My mom is a nurse, and she works in a hospital here in Louisville. My dad is currently unemployed.

I was going to tell Mom that I could get a baseball scholarship to college. But after my performance in the Little League World Series, that didn't seem very likely.

I looked up from my video game when I heard a car door slam in the driveway.

"You expecting anybody, Mom?" I asked.

We both got up to peek through the blinds. There was a guy getting out of the car. He looked like he was around 30 or so. Crew cut. He was wearing a black suit, black tie, and sunglasses; and he was carrying a black briefcase. His car was black too.

"He looks like an FBI agent," I whispered.

My mother giggled.

"Do you *really* think he could be an FBI agent?"

"Nah, can't be," I told her. "FBI agents only dress like FBI agents on TV. I bet *real* FBI agents dress like normal people so nobody will know they're FBI agents. This guy is probably selling insurance or something."

The guy jogged up the front steps. He looked like he worked out every day. My mom ran to wipe her hands on a dish towel and started fussing with her hair like she was getting ready to go out on a date or something.

When the guy knocked on the door, I opened it. He had taken off his sunglasses.

"Excuse me," the guy said politely. "Are you Joseph Stoshack?"

My mom stepped in front of me protectively.

She blocked the doorway like she didn't want this stranger coming into our house.

"Who wants to know?" she asked.

"Graham Pluto," he replied. "Federal Bureau of Investigation."

The guy *was* an FBI agent!

He flipped open his wallet and stuck his badge in our faces, just like they do on TV. It was a real badge too, not one of those phony plastic ones you can buy at a Halloween store. He looked serious.

Why would the FBI come to our house? We never did anything wrong.

Then it hit me. Flip had asked me to carry the flag at the Little League World Series, and I'd turned him down. I had committed an un-American act. I was totally unpatriotic, and stupid too. The FBI probably suspected that I was a terrorist.

"I'm really sorry!" I blurted out. "I didn't mean it! Really. I won't do it again."

"Do *what* again?" my mom asked.

My mind was racing. *This could ruin my whole life*, I thought to myself. *I'll never get through airport security again. I'm probably on a no-fly list already. It will be on my permanent record. I might go to jail. Or be deported. They might send me to one of those countries that tortures people to make them talk. I would never see my parents again.*

Flip must have tipped off the FBI about me not carrying the flag, I figured. Or maybe it was one of my teammates.

I felt like I might start to cry, but I fought against the tears.

"Did my son do something wrong?" Mom asked, tightening her hold on me.

"No, no, of course not!" Agent Pluto said, a tiny smile appearing above his square jaw for the first time. "May I come in, Mrs. Stoshack?"

"Of course."

Mom ushered Agent Pluto in and offered him coffee, tea, a sandwich, Fig Newtons, and just about everything she had in the refrigerator. But he said he just wanted to talk for a few minutes.

We went to the living room. I sat on the couch next to my mom, who held my hand. Agent Pluto sat stiffly on the wing chair across from us.

"Let me get right to the point, Joseph," he said. "We at the Bureau know about your . . . uh . . . shall we say . . . *gift.*"

I glanced at my mother, and she glanced back at me. Suddenly I felt hot. My forehead was sweaty.

"Gift?" Mom said innocently. "Did you get a birthday present that you didn't tell me about, Joey?"

"No."

"I'm really sorry," my mother said, "but we don't know what you're talking about, Mr. Pluto."

"I think you know *exactly* what I'm talking about, Mrs. Stoshack," Agent Pluto said. "Joseph, we know that you can travel through time using baseball cards."

I exhaled. I must have been holding it in for a long time.

17

He was right. The jig was up. I *can* travel through time with baseball cards.

Here's the story in a nutshell: Something must have happened to my brain when I was born. I remember picking up one of my dad's old baseball cards. I couldn't even read yet. After a few seconds, I felt this strange tingling sensation in the tips of my fingers. I dropped the card right away, but I was fascinated. When I picked the card up again, I held on to it, and the tingling sensation moved up my arm. It was a pleasant, buzzy feeling, but scary at the same time. I dropped the card again.

I kept experimenting in my room, and then one day I decided not to drop the card. As I held on to it, the tingling sensation moved across my body. I closed my eyes. I felt myself getting lighter, like I was being lifted up off my bed.

And then I was gone. *Poof!* When I opened my eyes, I was in another place, another time, another *year*.

A baseball card, I discovered, was like a plane ticket to me. It would take me to the year on the card.

I started going on adventures to the past. I met famous players like Babe Ruth, Jackie Robinson, and Roberto Clemente. But those are stories for another day.

At first, nobody else knew that I had this power. Then my mom had found out, of course. I told my dad, who lives in an apartment on the other side of

Louisville. I ended up telling Flip too. Only a few other people knew. But now this FBI agent knew. And if he knew, how many other people in the government knew? Maybe *hundreds*. The information must be in a database somewhere.

"How did you find out that Joey can travel through time with baseball cards?" my mother asked Agent Pluto.

"It's our job to find things out, Mrs. Stoshack," he said. "Gathering intelligence is what we do."

"If you're so good at finding stuff out," I asked, "then how come you didn't know about 9/11 before it happened?"

"Joey!" Mom scolded me. "It wasn't *his* fault. He was probably in high school when 9/11 happened."

"It's a fair question, Mrs. Stoshack," Agent Pluto said, "and I'll answer it. Joseph, the FBI is not infallible, unfortunately. We make mistakes. Sometimes bad mistakes. And yes, I was in school on 9/11—in New York City. I was in science class. I remember it very clearly. It was horrible. In fact, that was the reason I joined the Bureau in the first place. I wanted to help prevent *another* 9/11."

"So why are you here today?" my mother asked. "Why is the FBI interested in my son?"

Agent Pluto leaned forward in the chair and clasped his hands together. He lowered his voice slightly, as if there was somebody in the next room. My Uncle Wilbur was home, but he was upstairs sleeping.

"Time travel is a subject that has been of interest to our government for a long time," Agent Pluto said slowly. "We've spent a lot of money, and a lot of time, researching it."

"I'm not sure I like where this is going," my mother said.

"Please hear me out, Mrs. Stoshack. You can imagine how time travel could be used to our country's benefit. If we made a serious mistake sometime in the past, we might be able to correct it. Or we could go back and revise the historical record, just like you can revise a document on a computer. If there was something that happened in the past that we didn't like or approve of, maybe we could go back in time and do something so that thing never happened in the first place. Do you see? Time traveling could be a very valuable tool."

"In other words, you want my son to change history for you," my mother said, a worried look on her face.

"Not for *me*," Agent Pluto replied. "For America. You see, despite all the effort we've put into time-travel research, nothing productive has come out of it. Even our top scientists had come to the conclusion that time travel was a physical impossibility. Until now, of course."

He was looking at me.

"So you want me to go back in time?" I asked. "What do you want me to do, kill Hitler or something?"

"That's not a bad idea, Joseph," Agent Pluto said, chuckling.

"My son is not going to kill *anyone*," my mother said sternly. "Not even Hitler."

"Of course not," Agent Pluto said, smiling again. "The FBI would *never* send a child—or an adult—to assassinate anyone. We don't do those sorts of things."

"I got it," I said excitedly. "You want me to *prevent* an assassination, right? Is it John F. Kennedy? Or Abraham Lincoln?"

"Neither," Agent Pluto said. "It's bigger than that."

"Bigger?" I asked. "What could be bigger than preventing the assassination of the president?"

Agent Pluto looked me in the eyes.

"I'll try not to bore you, Joseph," he said. "But I need to give you a little history. In the spring of 1938, Hitler and the Nazis took over Austria. The next year they conquered Czechoslovakia and Poland, and World War II was on. In 1940, they swept over Denmark, Norway, Belgium, the Netherlands, Luxembourg, and France. The Nazis controlled most of continental Europe. They were bombing England. They had teamed up with Italy and Japan. Joseph, do you know what happened on December 7th, 1941?"

I thought for a minute. It didn't ring a bell. Agent Pluto opened his briefcase.

"Pearl Harbor," my mother said.

"That's right," he said, taking a newspaper article out of his briefcase and handing it to me.

I had learned a little bit about Pearl Harbor in

Social Studies. It was an American naval base in Hawaii, and it was attacked by Japan on that day. The next day America declared war on Japan, and we were in World War II.

"Wait a minute," Mom said, holding my hand tighter. "Are you expecting *my little boy* to prevent the attack on Pearl Harbor?"

"I'm not that little, Mom," I protested.

"Not prevent it, no," Agent Pluto corrected her. "You see, Joseph, it was a surprise attack. Nobody knew it was coming. If the president, Franklin Roosevelt, knew that Japan was going to attack Pearl Harbor on December 7th, we could have been ready and waiting for them. We would have blown those planes out of the sky like it was a turkey shoot."

I went to give the newspaper article back to Agent Pluto, but he told me to keep it.

"So you want me to go back in time and warn President Roosevelt that Pearl Harbor is going to be attacked?" I asked.

"Exactly," Agent Pluto said. "Joseph, do you have any idea how many lives would have been saved if our government had known in advance about the attack on Pearl Harbor in 1941?"

"No . . ."

Agent Pluto took a calculator out of his briefcase and started punching buttons.

"First of all," he said, "more than 2,400 American soldiers were killed at Pearl Harbor that day. If the attack had been prevented, we probably would not have dropped atomic bombs on Hiroshima and Nagasaki a few years later. Those bombs killed approximately 200,000 people. Furthermore, it's very possible that America would have never even entered the war if there had been no Pearl Harbor. And do you know how many American soldiers died in World War II? 416,000."

"Wow" was all I could say.

"You can change the world, Joseph," Agent Pluto said, looking at me seriously. He punched the final numbers into the calculator and held it up for me. "You can save . . . 618,400 lives."

He let that sink in for a moment.

"But isn't it going to be dangerous?" my mother asked. "I mean, what if Joey changes some little thing in the past, and it sets in motion a series of events that change things for the *worse*? What if he, uh, steps on a twig or something in 1941, and as a result millions of people died? I've read about that sort of thing in science fiction books."

Agent Pluto smiled.

"So have I," he said. "Joseph would have to be very careful. We would pick and choose what parts of the past he would change. That's why we've chosen a very simple two-part task for Joseph to complete. One: get to President Roosevelt. Two: warn him about Pearl Harbor. That's *it*. Then come right back home. And avoid stepping on any twigs along the way."

Up until now I had mostly traveled back in time because I was a baseball fan. I wanted to see if Babe

23

Ruth really called his famous "called-shot" home run. I wanted to see if Satchel Paige could throw 100 miles per hour.

I looked at my mom.

"How much would Joseph be paid for this . . . mission?" she asked.

A look of disappointment passed over Agent Pluto's face.

"Mom!" I exclaimed.

"We're not wealthy, Joseph," she said. "If you're the only person in the world who can do this, and you're going to risk your life for your country, you should get something out of it. That's only fair. This could pay for your college education."

"I'm sorry, Mrs. Stoshack, but we're not offering any money. Budgets . . . cutbacks . . . you understand."

"So you expect my son to save hundreds of thousands of lives and change the world to suit your purposes," my mom said, "but you're not willing to pay him a *dime*?"

"He gets to help his country in a way nobody else can," Agent Pluto said. "*That's* the payment. It's an honor to be asked to serve your country."

"I don't know," my mother said doubtfully. "He's just a boy."

"Joseph won't be working *alone*," said Agent Pluto. "Of course there would be adult supervision."

"Who?" I asked.

He reached into his briefcase again and pulled out a card that was in a clear plastic holder.

"I'm a big baseball fan myself," Agent Pluto told me as he put the card on the coffee table. "Love the game. I'll go see minor-league games, high school games, even Little League games if I'm in the mood."

I didn't pick the card up. I knew what would happen if I did.

It was black-and-white and larger than a regular baseball card. It was almost the size of a postcard. And it was autographed.

"Ted Williams?" I asked.

I didn't know a whole lot about Williams. He was

He put the card on the coffee table.

25

a great hitter, of course. Everybody knows that. He played for the Red Sox. He's in the Hall of Fame. That's about it.

"You could have chosen *any* player from that era," my mother said. "What's so special about Ted Williams?"

"We've done extensive personality research on the players from decades past," Agent Pluto told us. "We have reason to believe that of all the players in the Major Leagues, Ted Williams would be most likely to help Joseph carry out this mission."

Agent Pluto stood up, pulled out his wallet, and removed a business card. He handed it to my mother.

"I don't expect you folks to make a snap decision about this," he said. "I understand the risks that are involved. But think it over. Call me and let me know what you decide to do. And this is top secret, obviously. Not a word about this to anybody."

"What if we say no?" my mom asked. "Will this go on Joseph's permanent record?"

"Of course not," Agent Pluto said simply. "There are no repercussions. We just thought that, if Joseph is traveling through time anyway, he might want to do something to help his country."

Mom and I walked him to the front door. He put his sunglasses on. When I opened the door, he turned to face me.

"Joseph," he said, "I told you that I joined the FBI to prevent another 9/11. Pearl Harbor was the *first* 9/11. In just two hours on that day, 21 American ships were sunk or damaged. Over 300 planes were destroyed. And besides those 2,400 soldiers who were killed, more than 1,200 were wounded. A lot of those guys were teenagers, not much older than you. Keep that in mind when you make your decision."

"I will," I said.

"And, Joseph," he added before leaving, "this is just my opinion, but you really should have carried that flag in the World Series."

3

Flip

I LET OUT A DEEP BREATH WHEN THE FBI AGENT LEFT THE house.

So I had a decision to make. Should I use my power to go back to 1941 and warn the president about Pearl Harbor, save the lives of all those people, and change history forever? Or should I say no?

Up until now I pretty much went back in time for *me*. I wanted to meet Ruth, Paige, Shoeless Joe Jackson, Jackie Robinson, and all those other players. This time I would be doing it for my country.

It would be dangerous, of course. In my previous trips through time, I had been shot at, kidnapped, locked in a closet, tied to a chair, chased by a crazed batboy, and punched by a Pittsburgh Pirate fan. One time I landed in the middle of a *war*. Who knew what I might encounter this time?

What if I got blown off course somehow and ended

up in Pearl Harbor on Pearl Harbor Day, with bombs and torpedoes all around me? That would suck.

There was one person I needed to talk to before I made my decision: Flip Valentini.

I know, I should probably have talked to my dad about something so important. He does know a lot about baseball. Not as much as Flip, but he knows a lot. And he is my dad, after all. You're supposed to go to your dad for advice. He was the one who got me interested in collecting baseball cards in the first place.

But no, not my dad. All he cares about are two things, and the first one is the Yankees. The Yankees and Red Sox have always been big rivals, so he wouldn't be happy to hear I was going to meet Ted Williams. He would probably try to talk me into going to see Joe DiMaggio or one of the great Yankees from that era instead.

The other thing my dad cares about is money, which is kind of odd because he never seems to have any. He would probably ask me to have Ted Williams sign a bunch of autographs so he could sell them. My dad does stuff like that.

I rode my bike over to Flip's store. It's in a strip mall on Shelbyville Road. The little bell jingled as I opened the door. Flip greeted me with a big smile when I walked inside. He seemed to have forgotten what I did at the Little League World Series. Or if he remembered, it didn't bother him anymore.

Flip's Fan Club is jammed with all kinds of

baseball cards, memorabilia, and junk. There was a lot of new stuff I hadn't seen before. I picked up a Beatles bobblehead statue and Flip laughed.

"I'm diversifyin'," he explained. "Baby boomers wanna buy collectibles—junk they shoulda held on to when they were young."

"Not many kids collect cards anymore," I said.

Flip was holding a copy of *Discover* magazine.

"Yo, Stosh, y'ever hear of a Dr. Anton Zeilinger?"

"No."

"He's an Austrian physicist," Flip told me. "Says here that he destroyed bits of light and made perfect copies appear three feet away. Ha! He thinks we'll be able to do teleportation between atoms in a few years and molecules within a decade."

"That's ridiculous," I told him. "Everybody knows that's impossible."

Flip chuckled and took off his reading glasses. He's had a special interest in time travel ever since I took him back to 1948 with me. You see, Flip had been a pretty decent ballplayer himself when he was a teenager. But he got *real* good after I took him to 1948 and Satchel Paige taught him a few trick pitches. Flip ended up getting stuck back then and had to live his life all over again. The good part was that in his second chance at life, he made it into the majors.

But that's a story for another day.

"What can I do ferya?" he asked me.

"Flip, would you mind locking the door for a few

minutes?" I asked.

"Sure, Stosh," Flip said. "Somethin' wrong?"

"I've got a secret," I confided.

"Do tell."

"Flip, the FBI knows," I told him.

"They know *what*?" he asked.

"They know about *me*," I explained. "They know what I can do with baseball cards. They sent one of their agents over to my house to talk to me."

Flip looked concerned.

"How did they find out?" he asked.

"I don't know," I told him. "The guy was all mysterious about it."

Flip sighed and took a sip from his coffee mug.

"I was afraid this was gonna happen," he told me. "What do they want from you?"

"They want me to go on a mission."

"Jesus," Flip said. "That's bad news. The FBI shouldn't be messin' with kids. What kinda mission?"

"They want me to go back to 1941 and warn President Roosevelt about the attack on Pearl Harbor."

"Are you kiddin' me?" Flip said, getting out of his chair. He looked really angry.

"I wish I was kidding."

Flip whistled and sat back down.

"This is big, Stosh. Real big."

"The FBI guy told me that if the president knew about Pearl Harbor in advance, we would have been able to just blow those planes out of the sky," I said. "Like it was a turkey shoot."

Flip leaned back and gazed off into space for a moment. It looked like he was thinking about a distant memory.

"Smart," he said. "Obviously. You'd save a lotta lives. If there hadn't been a Pearl Harbor, it woulda changed everything."

"Do you remember that day, Flip?" I asked him. "December 7th, 1941?"

"Sure," he said, still with that faraway look. "I was a kid. 'Bout your age, I guess. Heard about it on the radio. It was a Sunday morning. My next-door neighbor was stationed in Hawaii. Joey Albanese. Good guy. He used to play ball with me and my friends. I never even hearda Pearl Harbor until that day. None of us had. And then it happened. Joey got killed with all the others. They never found his body. It was 9/11 for my generation."

I had never seen Flip cry, not even when we lost a really tough game. But I could see that his eyes were watery when he remembered his friend. Suddenly, a plan popped into my brain.

"Hey, I can save your friend Joey's life, Flip!" I said excitedly. "I can go back to 1941 and prevent the attack on Pearl Harbor. Then when I get back here, maybe Joey will still be alive! I can bring him back to life! What do you think?"

Flip looked at me for a long time and then got that faraway look in his eyes again.

"No," he said, shaking his head. "Don't do it, Stosh."

4

Kill Three Birds with One Stone

I NEVER EXPECTED TO HEAR FLIP DISCOURAGE ME FROM doing what I do with baseball cards. He never had any reservations before. Flip had always been my biggest supporter.

"Leave well enough alone, Stosh," he told me. "Pearl Harbor's over. It's history. Let it go. In the long run, things worked out okay."

"Are you saying the attack on Pearl Harbor was a *good* thing?" I asked him.

"Yeah . . . sorta," Flip said. "Look, a lotta people didn't want us to get into that war, Stosh. If we hadn't been attacked, we never woulda jumped in. We woulda stood on the sideline and let the rest of the world knock their brains out."

"What's wrong with that?" I asked. "It sounds like a good thing to me."

"Stosh, if we hadn't entered the war, we probably wouldn't have built the atomic bomb. If he hadn't built the A-bomb, the Nazis woulda eventually. You could bet on that. And Hitler woulda used it too, to win the war. He woulda conquered the world. That's why Pearl Harbor was so important. It got us in the war. And that's why we won it."

"But you don't know all that stuff for sure," I said.

"Course not," Flip said. "Nobody knows nothin' for sure. I'm just spitballin'. But if you came in here looking for a 1941 card to use, I can't give you one. My conscience won't let me."

"I didn't come here to get a card, Flip," I told him. "The FBI guy already gave me one."

"Who's on it?" Flip asked.

"Ted Williams," I replied. "Can you give me a crash course on him? Just so I know what I'm getting into?"

Flip smiled a little.

"Stosh, I think I can sum up Ted Williams with one word," Flip said. "And that word is . . . 'jerk.'"

"He was a *jerk*?"

"A real jerk," Flip said. "Williams had anger problems. He was always gettin' into beefs with everybody: players, managers, reporters, fans. He would throw bats, tear out the plumbing, punch the water cooler, knock out the lights. He'd spit at people. Go look it up if ya don't believe me."

"I believe you," I said.

"But could that guy hit a baseball!" Flip shook his

head in wonder. "Probably the greatest pure hitter ever. Oh, Cobb hit for a higher average. And Ruth had more power. But overall, *nobody* was better than Williams. If you ask me, he was the greatest hitter ever."

Flip reached under the counter, pulled out a thick book, and flipped through the pages until he found the section on Ted Williams. Flip loves statistics. He put his reading glasses back on.

"Look at this," Flip said. "Lifetime average, .344. Career homers, 521. He won the batting title *six* times, and the last time when he was forty years

The greatest hitter ever.

old. Oldest guy ever to do that. He won the Triple Crown twice, and the MVP twice. He led the American League in slugging percentage nine times, total bases six times, runs scored six times, and walks eight times. And get this—he only struck out 709 times in his whole career. Ya know how many times Reggie Jackson struck out?"

"I give up."

"2,597!"

"How did he do in 1941," I asked. "That was the year of Pearl Harbor."

"It was his greatest season," Flip told me. "That was the year he hit .400. Or .406 to be exact."

He dug up a newspaper article from a drawer and handed it to me. The headline read: "Batting Mark of .4057 for Williams."

"Nobody's done it since then, y'know," Flip continued. "Williams was the last guy to hit .400. That's more than seventy years ago. And he *still* didn't win the MVP that year. That's how much everybody hated him."

Flip closed the book with a thud.

"Why do you think the FBI picked Ted Williams?" I asked. "They could have picked *any* ballplayer from 1941."

"I think I know why," Flip said, pulling out a photo from a file. "Williams was a military guy. A fighter pilot in the marines. In fact, he served in *two* wars: World War II and Korea. Altogether, he gave up almost five years of his baseball career to serve his country."

"Five years?" I asked. "And you said he hit 521 homers? How could he hit that many homers when he missed so many games?"

"That's how good he was," Flip said.

Ted Williams was a fighter pilot in the marines.

"How many homers do you think he would have hit if he hadn't been in the military for those five years?" I asked.

"That's the million-dollar question," Flip said, his eyes flashing. "I'll tell you this much. Williams enlisted when he was 24 years old. When Mickey Mantle was 24, he hit 52 homers. When Willie Mays was 24, he hit 51. When Jimmie Foxx was 24, he hit 58. So it's a good bet that Williams woulda hit 50 or more that year, and the next few years too. Ruth hit 714 in his career. With five more seasons and a little luck, Williams could have beaten that. 'Course, we'll never know for sure. . . ."

Flip looked up at me, and I looked back at him. We were both thinking the same thing. I could go back in time and talk Ted Williams out of joining the military. If he had those seasons back, he would have hit a lot more homers, maybe enough to beat Babe Ruth.

"Flip," I said, "I'm gonna do it."

Flip wrinkled his forehead as he put the book away.

"I don't like this, Stosh," he said. "Williams had a great career, one of the greatest ever. What's done is done. You don't need to change history."

"But I can make his career even *greater*," I told Flip, "and I can warn the president about the attack on Pearl Harbor. Plus, I can save your friend. That's killing three birds with one stone."

"What if *you* get killed, Stosh?" Flip said, shaking his head. "Like I told you, you're the son I never had."

"Don't worry about me," I assured him. "I'll be fine."

5

The Point of No Return

I could save all those lives by warning President Roosevelt about the attack on Pearl Harbor. And if the war happened anyway, America and its allies probably would have won it with or without Ted Williams, I figured. One man doesn't win a war. So it probably wouldn't matter to the war effort if I were to talk Williams into staying home and playing baseball. He would hit lots more homers in his career and maybe even more than Babe Ruth.

But on the bike ride home from Flip's store, I began to have second thoughts about the mission. I hate when that happens. You decide to do something, and then you start thinking about it. And the more you think about it, the more you think of all the reasons why you shouldn't do it.

What if Flip was right? What if preventing Pearl Harbor would keep America out of the war and the

Nazis built an atomic bomb before we did? They would take over the world. And it would all be *my* fault.

Plus, Flip told me that Ted Williams was a jerk that spit on people. Why would I want to help a guy like that get even more famous than he already was?

As I rode my bike home, my mind kept going back and forth.

It might be dangerous, I thought.

But the FBI asked me to do it.

I might get stuck in 1941 forever, I thought.

But I could become a national hero.

I might get killed, I thought.

But I'd get to meet Ted Williams.

My brain was being pushed and pulled in all different directions.

When I got home, my mother was still at work. Good. I wouldn't have to get into a big debate with her over the whole thing. And if I did decide to go on the mission, my mom wouldn't be around to nag me about bringing along lunch, an umbrella, a first aid kit, or any junk like that.

I grabbed a snack and tiptoed upstairs, trying to be quiet so I wouldn't wake my uncle Wilbur. He's really old and naps a lot of the time.

The baseball card that Agent Pluto gave me was on my bed. I didn't pick it up. Not yet. I knew what would happen once I picked it up.

Rummaging through the drawer of my night table, I found a new pack of baseball cards and put it in my pocket—just in case. They would be my ticket home.

I still hadn't made up my mind. I looked at the Williams card, turning it over with a pencil to look at the back. It was probably very rare. The FBI must have paid a lot of money for it. Agent Pluto never asked for it back, so I had to assume it was mine to keep. Maybe Flip could appraise it for me. Maybe he would even buy it off me.

Out of the corner of my eye, I saw something moving in the hallway. It was Uncle Wilbur in his wheelchair. He stopped in the doorway.

"A penny for your thoughts, Joey," he said.

Uncle Wilbur and I didn't have a lot in common. But we did have a special bond. I saved his life once.

What happened was that I went back to 1919 to meet Shoeless Joe Jackson. I had the flu that day, and I brought my medicine with me. As it happened, I bumped into my great-great-uncle Wilbur. Well, he wasn't Uncle Wilbur yet. He was just a kid in 1919, and he was sick with the flu. They didn't have flu medicine in those days, and millions of people died in an epidemic that year. Uncle Wilbur would have been one of them, but I gave him my flu medicine. And when I got back to my own time, I was astonished to find Uncle Wilbur was alive—an old man who had survived the flu epidemic of 1919. He owed his whole life to me.

"Oh," I said while he sat in the doorway. "I didn't see you there."

"It looked like you were thinking about something pretty hard," he said.

I told him the whole story about the FBI agent coming over to talk about Pearl Harbor and how Flip had advised me not to go.

"What do *you* think I should do?" I asked.

Uncle Wilbur thought it over for a minute, and then he wheeled himself closer to my bed.

"I've been around for nearly a century, Joey," he told me, "and in my whole life, I have only one regret."

"What's that?"

"When I was a teenager, a few years older than you," he said, "there was this girl I liked. Well, I loved her, to tell you the truth. Beautiful girl. Cammy, her name was. Cammy Provorny. Her dad was a lawyer. She didn't know I was in love with her. I never said a word. I thought a girl like that would never be interested in me. She was out of my league, y'know? And I was scared to ask her to go on a date. I didn't want her to laugh in my face. I didn't want to have to see her after she turned me down. So I never did anything about it."

"That's sad," I said.

"And to this day, Joey, every day I think about Cammy Provorny. I think about how my life might have been different if I had simply asked her to go for a walk with me. Maybe we would have hit it off. We might have gotten married. We might have raised a family, and I might have had a son like you. You never know."

"And you never got married to anybody?" I asked.

"I never met another girl that made me feel the way Cammy did," Uncle Wilbur said. "You only live once, Joey. That's all I'm saying. And you miss a hundred percent of the shots you don't take. You know who said that?"

"Uh . . . Michael Jordan?" I guessed.

"Wayne Gretzky."

Uncle Wilbur rolled back out of the room. I closed the door behind him and sat back down on my bed.

I don't want to be a sad old man someday, looking back on my life and wondering what might have happened if I had done things differently. I don't want to have regrets.

I picked up the Williams card. It was in a clear plastic holder. I squeezed the holder in the middle and the card slipped out, fluttering onto the floor. I leaned over and picked it up.

Nothing happened at first. It never does. I closed my eyes and thought about Ted Williams. Maybe he *was* a jerk. Maybe he was a nice guy. But I wouldn't know from some old book or someone's old memories. I would find out on my own.

It didn't take long, maybe a minute or two. There was a gentle buzzy feeling in my fingertips. It was sort of like a cat purring. It felt nice.

After a short time, the feeling started to move. Up my arm. Across my shoulder. Down my back. There was a whooshing sound in my ears, as if air was passing through my head.

I was starting to feel light-headed. It was like I was entering weightlessness. I lay back on my pillow. The tingling feeling was on my other side now, and I could begin to feel it moving down my legs.

This must be what it's like to be hypnotized, I thought. To be in a trance. To meditate.

I reached the point where I couldn't drop the card even if I wanted to. It was like when you pass the halfway point in a trip, and it would take longer to turn back and drive home than it would to keep going to your destination. The point of no return.

I felt like I was giving off a glow, but I didn't dare open my eyes to see it.

The indentation made by my body in the bed was smoothing out. I was getting lighter. Everything was starting to vibrate. The tingling sensation was all over me. I took a deep breath, like I was about to swim underwater.

And then I disappeared.

6

Oh, !@#$%!

When I opened my eyes, I was flat on my stomach in near darkness surrounded by piles of junk. There was a loud roaring all around me—like the sound of a jet engine—and everything was vibrating. I didn't see a window, so I couldn't tell where I was. It was freezing cold. I felt like I might be locked in the trunk of a really old car.

What was I doing *here*?

In the dim light, I squinted to look at the stuff scattered around me. There was a flashlight, a whistle, a Swiss army knife, a compass, some flares, a first aid kit, and a bottle of shark repellent. *Shark repellent?!* This was survival gear. The cover of the map had one word on it: "KOREA." That's when I realized what was going on.

I was in a *plane*.

Something must have gone horribly wrong. All

the other times I had traveled through time with a baseball card, I wound up somewhere near the player on the card. But now I was up in the air, going who knows where. *I should have taken Flip's advice,* I said to myself. This was a big mistake.

It had to be a very small plane. A couple of feet in front of me was the back of the pilot's seat. I could see the top of his helmet, and I crawled about five feet forward toward him. There wasn't a lot of room because of the stuff all over. With the noise from the engines, I guess he didn't hear me.

"Uh, excuse me . . ." I said, tapping the pilot on his shoulder.

"Holy !@#$%!" he said, jumping even though he was strapped tightly into his seat. "Who the !@#$%! are you?"

The guy sure had a mouth on him. I'd heard the curse words before, of course, but most grown-ups try to watch their language around kids. I couldn't blame him, though. If I was flying a plane by myself and some kid came out of nowhere and suddenly tapped me on the shoulder, I would freak out too.

The pilot turned his head around to look at me. He looked familiar. He had curly dark hair under his helmet and bushy eyebrows.

"M-My name is J-Joe Stoshack," I stammered. "I'm a—"

"You're a *kid*!" he shouted in my face, his voice booming. "How the !@#$%! did you get in here?"

"I . . . don't know," I sputtered. "It was an accident.

I—I didn't mean to. I just—who are *you*?"

"Captain Theodore Williams," he replied. "United States Marines."

I just about lost it. Of *course* he looked familiar to me. He looked just like the photos I had seen of him.

"You're Ted Williams?"

"Look, Junior," he replied. "I got no time for chit-chat and autographs. I don't know how you got in here, but I have a mission to accomplish. So sit back and keep your mouth shut. I'll deal with you after we land. "

He turned back around to scan the sky in front of him. He was controlling the plane with a stick, sort of like the joysticks they have in video game arcades.

"I have a mission to accomplish too," I told him. "I live in the twenty-first century, and I can travel through time with baseball cards. I came here to warn President Roosevelt about Pearl Harbor. I'm going to prevent the attack—"

"Pearl Harbor? Roosevelt?" Ted said, turning around to look at me again. The words exploded from his mouth. "Are you out of your !@#$%! mind? Roosevelt has been *dead* for eight years!"

"That's impossible!" I shouted. "What year is it?"

"Give me a break, Junior," Ted said. "It's 1953. Pearl Harbor happened 12 years ago. That war is long over. They found us a *new* war to fight."

I rooted around on the floor until I found the Ted Williams card I had used to get there. I always travel to the year on the card. But looking at it closely, I couldn't find a year printed on it anywhere.

I realized what had happened. The FBI agent must have given me a 1953 card instead of a 1941 card! I never bothered to check it. I just assumed FBI agents knew what they were doing. After all, they're the FBI!

"Is this the Vietnam War?" I asked Ted.

"Vietnam?" he shouted back at me. "What the !@#$%! are you talking about? We're in Korea, Junior. Look, I'm gonna say this just one time, so listen up good. Once we get over the target in Kyiomipo, I'm gonna be dropping a 3,000-pound load of napalm on a Commie supply center. Then we hightail it out of there. Got it? I got no time for babysitting, so keep your mouth shut and let me do my job. My opinion is not open to debate!"

"Yes, sir."

I pushed myself forward until I was right behind the pilot's seat. Now I could see out the canopy window. It was a bright, clear day with a few clouds in the sky. On our left and right, there were lots of other American bombers flying alongside us. There could have been *dozens* of them. If all those planes were going to be dropping bombs, I wouldn't want to be on the ground looking up.

We continued for the next few minutes in tense silence, with Ted talking pilot mumbo jumbo into his radio to the other planes. I had a lot of questions to ask, but I didn't want to get him angry, so I kept quiet.

"It's time," he finally said. "Find something to hold on to, Junior. We're going in, and this could get a little bumpy."

I grabbed a handle on the wall next to me. He pushed the stick forward. The nose of the plane tilted down, and we went into a dive. It was a really steep angle. The engines roared. For a moment, I felt weightless as we dropped through the clouds. If I hadn't been holding on, the g-force would have pushed me against the ceiling. On the dashboard—or whatever you call it on a plane—the altimeter dipped below 2,000 feet. I felt my ears pop. I could see the ground coming up at us. Ted pushed a button, and there was a rumbling sound coming from below.

"Bomb bay doors open!" Ted shouted into the radio. "I'm north of the 38th parallel, 15 miles from Pyongyang. Bombs away!"

Ted pushed another button, and a moment later I felt the plane swoop upward. I was pressed against the floor now. He must have dropped his bombs, and that made the plane a lot lighter. I heard a sound like bullets hitting metal.

"Too low," Ted mumbled.

"What's happening?" I shouted.

"They're shooting at us!" he barked. "What the !@#$%! do you expect? You shoot at them, and they get to shoot back. That's why they call it war."

We were banking into a turn now as if we were making a run for it. There was a beeping sound, and I looked over Ted's shoulder to see lights flashing on the dashboard.

"What does that mean?" I asked hesitantly.

"The wheels are down," he replied.

"Is that bad?"

"It is if you're not about to land," he said. "The hydraulics may be leaking. We took some flak back there."

Ted pressed some more buttons, and the wheels came back up. He breathed a sigh of relief, but then the stick he was using to control the plane began to shake wildly in his hand.

"What does that mean?" I asked.

"Will you shut the !@#$%! up, Junior?" he shouted back at me. "You wanna *die* here?"

Ted began yelling into the radio, trying to contact the other pilots.

"Antiaircraft fire! We've been hit! Plane is wounded. Mayday! I'm hit! The radio is dead."

Every light was flashing red, and the dashboard was blinking like a Christmas tree. I could see buttons labeled LOW FUEL and FIRE.

Oh, no. I had been in some tough situations before, but not like *this*. I had even been shot at before but never while I was in danger of falling out of the *sky*.

I knew traveling through time would catch up with me eventually. Something bad was bound to happen. It was just a matter of time. I felt tears welling up in my eyes.

"Are we going to die?" I asked quietly.

"It's a distinct possibility," Ted said as the plane

leveled off. "I gotta abort the flight plan. We need to get over some water, fast. I'm heading for the Yellow Sea. I may have to hit the silk."

He took off his leg straps and seat belt.

"Hit the silk? You mean eject?" I asked. "We're going to parachute out?"

"No, *I'm* gonna parachute out," he said. You think I carry two parachutes in case unexpected company shows up? You'll be on your own, Junior. Good luck."

"You can't leave me here to die!" I shouted, and then I let the tears come. I didn't care if he heard me cry.

"Oh, !@#$%!" Ted turned around and locked his eyes with mine. "Leave it to me, Junior. I'll find a way out of this."

When I looked in his eyes, I didn't see panic. Just the opposite, in fact. It was like a sense of calm had come over him. Most people freak out when they're in a stressful situation. With Ted Williams, the stress seemed to focus his attention on solving the problem at hand. I may have been about to die, but for some reason I felt safe with him at the controls.

My nose and ears were stuffed up, but I could still smell something burning. Jet fuel? Were the tires on fire? Or was it something else? I tried to regain my composure. I looked out the window at the water on the left. Ted was looking out there too.

"It's frozen," he said. "I'm not jumping outta this thing onto ice. I'd break every !@#$%! bone in my body. Not *this* boy."

On the right side, I saw another American bomber pulling up alongside us. He was so close, I could see the pilot making frantic hand gestures at Ted.

"What's he saying?" I asked.

"He says I'm leaking fuel," Ted replied. "We're not gonna be able to make it back to base. We gotta land somewhere else."

The pilot of the other plane signaled for Ted to follow him. Ted replied with an OK sign and turned in the same direction.

"Can anybody hear me?" he shouted into the radio. "I've got a wounded duck. One of my fuel lines has been hit."

"What does that mean?" I asked, not sure I wanted to hear the answer.

The pilot was signaling for Ted to follow him.

"This is an F-9 Panther with a centrifugal-flow engine," Ted explained. "When it gets hit, the tail usually blows off. If that happens, you'll get sucked out of there. And if the fuel pools at the bottom of the engine, you can kiss your !@#$%! good-bye, 'cause we're gonna blow up."

"Oh, great!" I said, cursing my luck. "What are you gonna do?"

But it was obvious what he was going to do. The other pilot went into a steep climb, and Ted followed him. Clouds were shooting past the window like signs on the highway.

"He's taking me higher," Ted said. "Fire can't burn in thin air. If we get high enough, we can glide 30 or 40 miles without the engines. Then maybe we can find a place to land."

The altimeter said we had leveled off at 25,000 feet. Ted took off his oxygen mask and told me he was going to turn off the hydraulics and try to steer manually.

"Can you land it?" I asked.

"We're gonna find out, now aren't we?" he replied. "In case I can't, it's been nice knowing you, Junior."

I said a silent prayer and tried to adjust my position so that I would be able to absorb the biggest possible impact when we landed. I noticed a trickle of blood coming out of Ted's right ear.

"There's blood coming out of your ear," I told him.

"I know," he replied. "It happens at high altitude. It's my sinuses."

We followed the other plane for a few minutes and then the pilot turned slightly. Ted followed. We were slowly coming down. I didn't say anything.

"We crossed the border," Ted said. "We're in South Korea now. At least nobody will be shooting at us anymore. He's leading me to another base. Looks like Suwon. K-13."

We continued gliding down, much more slowly. It was strangely quiet without the engines roaring. I wasn't sure if Ted had turned them off or if we had leaked all our fuel. I just hoped we had been high enough to glide all the way down. Ted was pulling on the stick like he was trying to hold on to a bucking bronco.

"The !@#$%! flaps don't work," he said. "The wheels won't come down. If one of the wings comes off, we're finished. You holding on to anything, Junior?"

"Yeah."

The altimeter was dropping. 7,500 feet. 5,600 feet. 3,200 feet. 2,000 feet.

Suddenly, it occurred to me that I didn't have to sit there and let fate determine what was going to happen to me. I had a pack of new baseball cards with me! I could go back to my own time whenever I wanted. Holding on to the handle with one hand, I used the other one to fish around in my pockets. But I couldn't find it.

Looking out the canopy window in front, I could see what looked to be a landing strip in the distance. There were rows and rows of other planes on the ground. The only other plane in the air was the one that was escorting us down.

The pilot of that plane signaled for Ted to lower his wheels. But when Ted pushed a button on the dashboard to do that, there was an explosion that shook the whole plane.

"!@#$%!" Ted muttered.

"What happened?" I yelled.

"One of the !@#$%! wheel doors blew off!" he yelled back to me. "When we reduced our speed, it must have made the fuel pool up in the wheel wells."

There was a whooshing sound behind me; and when I turned around, all I could see were flames.

"We're on fire!" I yelled. "We've got to eject!"

"Too late for that," Ted shouted back. "We're gonna have to crash-land this bucket of bolts, Junior."

"I'm gonna die!" I screamed. "Of all the ways you could die! I never thought—"

"Will you shut up?" Ted yelled. "I'm trying to concentrate! We've got about 11,000 feet of runway to slide on."

"Is that long enough?" I asked.

"We're about to find out."

He looked calm, totally calm and focused. I grabbed the handles tighter. Even if I could find my baseball cards now, it might be too late to use one. We were coming in low, just barely clearing a fence that surrounded the base.

"Here goes nothin'!" Ted hollered as we were about to touch ground.

If the speedometer was working properly, we hit the runway at 225 miles per hour. It felt nothing like the few other times I had been on a plane. With no wheels, we hit the ground belly first, with a bump that bounced me a foot off the floor. I was still holding the handles on the sides. There was the awful sound of metal scraping against pavement. Everything was shaking. My teeth were vibrating in my mouth. I was afraid they were going to fall out.

Ted mashed his foot on the brake and was pulling on the stick, but it wasn't doing anything. We just had to let physics run its course—deceleration, momentum, and all those laws Newton figured out centuries ago.

Pieces of the plane were flying off as we scraped along the runway. I could see flames, sparks, smoke, and debris out the back, because that part of the plane wasn't there anymore. In the distance, I heard the siren from fire trucks speeding toward the runway.

"Stop, you dirty !@#$%!" Ted was shouting. "When is this dirty son of a !@#$%! gonna stop? If there's a Christ, this is the time old Teddy Ballgame needs you!"

It felt like we were sliding along the ground *forever*. I was hoping and praying that we wouldn't run out of runway.

In front of us, I could see rice paddies and a Korean village. What a stupid place for there to be a village! Women and children were running for their lives to get out of the way.

We slid off the runway, a little to the left. By that time, we had slowed down quite a bit, and the dirt and grass slowed us down even more. But we were still moving when Ted pulled an emergency lever to pop the cockpit canopy open. It flew off behind us. I felt the rush of air on my face.

"Get out, Junior!" Ted shouted. "There still might be enough fuel left in this junker to blow!"

The plane—or what was left of it, anyway—finally came to a stop just past the end of the runway. Ted somersaulted out of the hatch and rolled off to the right, out of sight.

Acrid smoke filled my nose. The whole plane was in flames. The sleeve of my shirt was on fire! I jumped out, rolled a few times, and landed in a ditch on the opposite side of the plane from Ted.

I had survived.

As I lay in the ditch catching my breath, I planned my next move. *I could stay here,* I thought. Ted might take care of me. But what would be the point? It was 1953. I couldn't stop Pearl Harbor, because it was already years in the past. And I couldn't talk Ted out of joining the marines, because he was obviously already *in* the marines. I might as well try to get home.

I fumbled around in my pockets again for my base-ball cards. *There* they were! I ripped the pack open and pulled out a card. Fire trucks had arrived on the other side of the plane, and somebody was shooting foam stuff to snuff out the flames. But nobody could see me in the ditch.

I closed my eyes and tried to put what happened out of my mind. I thought about going home. Back to the twenty-first century. Back to my house, where I would be safe. My own time.

It didn't take long. Soon I was feeling the tingling sensation in my fingertips. I breathed a sigh of relief. It was working. The buzzy feeling worked its way up my arm, across my chest, and down the other side. I began to feel light-headed, and I knew from experience that soon I would be gone.

And then I disappeared.

7

A Little Incentive

THE NEXT THING I KNEW I WAS FLYING ACROSS MY LIVING room, tripping over the coffee table, and almost slamming headfirst into the TV. I swerved out of the way at the last instant, landing on the floor next to the couch.

I was all messed up. Nothing was broken as far as I could tell. But I had scrapes on my arms, and I was sore all over. My head hurt.

I looked up and saw my mom and that FBI agent, Mr. Pluto. He was holding his briefcase; but he dropped it when he saw me, and they both came running over. My mom had tears on her face.

"Joey!" she screamed. "You're safe!"

"I'm sorry, Joseph," said Agent Pluto. "I came over as soon as I realized—"

His voice trailed off because my mom had stopped crying suddenly. She was examining me very closely, sniffing me.

"Joseph, you smell like smoke," she said sternly. "Have you been smoking?"

"Smoking?!" I said. "Yes, of *course* I was smoking! That's what you do when you're on *fire!*"

I turned to Agent Pluto and just about lost it.

"You didn't send me to 1941!" I yelled at him. "You sent me to 1953! Did you know that Ted Williams was a fighter pilot in the Korean War? I was in a plane with him! We got hit by anti-aircraft fire and had to crash-land!"

"I'm terribly sorry," Agent Pluto said, and he looked like he meant it. My mother was back in crying mode again.

"It was the *wrong year!*" I shouted at Pluto. "The wrong war! I risked my life! You almost got me killed! Don't you research this stuff in advance before you send people out on a dangerous mission? You're supposed to be the *FBI!*"

"I accept full responsibility for the error," Agent Pluto said, trying to calm me down. "We're not infallible. As soon as I realized that I had given you the wrong baseball card, I rushed over here. But you had already left. . . ."

"You're !@#$%! right you gave me the wrong card!" I shouted.

"Joseph!" my mother said. "Where did you learn such language?"

"From Ted Williams," I told her.

It took a few minutes for me to regain my composure.

I had been through a lot that day. Mom went to get me a glass of milk and came back with a plate filled with cookies too. I have to admit, the milk and cookies made me feel better. Mom got an ice pack from the freezer to put on my scrapes and bruises. The three of us sat down on the couch.

Agent Pluto took a card out of his jacket pocket and placed it carefully on the coffee table. This one looked more like a traditional old-time baseball card, with a cheesy illustration on the front. . . .

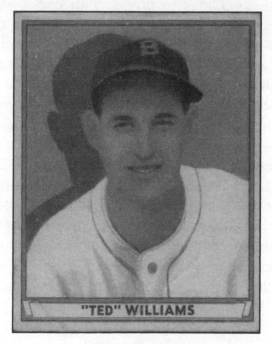

The 1941 card.

"*This* is the 1941 Ted Williams card," he said.

"You're sure now?" my mother asked, shooting him a look as she picked up the card to examine it.

"We've researched this card extensively to make sure it's authentic," Agent Pluto told us. "It was produced by a company called Gum Inc. and was part of their Play Ball series. The series was discontinued when World War II started."

"Why?" my mom asked.

"Every scrap of paper was needed for the war effort," he replied. "So no baseball cards were produced during that time. This card would have been sold as a penny pack. A kid would buy a wax paper pack for a penny and get a baseball card along with a square piece of gum."

"I wonder how much it's worth today," I asked.

"Hundreds," Agent Pluto replied, "especially the Williams and DiMaggio cards."

I knew that 1941 wasn't *just* the year Ted Williams hit .406. It was also the year Joe DiMaggio had his famous 56-game hitting streak. Neither record has been seriously challenged in over seventy years.

"So this card should work?" my mother asked.

"It will take Joseph to *sometime* in 1941," said Agent Pluto. "We can't say exactly when, of course. But we know Pearl Harbor was late in the year: December 7th. So chances are Joseph will arrive in 1941 *before* the attack. That will give him time to warn the president."

"I'm going to be very honest with you," my mother

62

said, a worried look on her face. "I don't feel good about this. Maybe what happened the first time was an omen. What if something *else* goes wrong next time? What if Joey lands at Pearl Harbor *exactly* on December 7th, and planes are dropping bombs all around him?"

"I would advise Joseph to abort the mission if he arrives on or after December 7th," Agent Pluto said. "He should just pull out one of his new baseball cards and return home immediately."

The two of them were talking back and forth as if I wasn't even there.

"What happens if I open my eyes and I'm inside a plane again?" I asked. "Or in a submarine or something?"

"I realize this is still a dangerous mission, and both of you have every right to be concerned," Agent Pluto said, turning to face me. "That's why I went back to the Bureau with a special request, which my superior granted. Here's the deal. We're willing to offer you a reward this time if the mission is carried out successfully."

He went over to get his briefcase and put it on the coffee table. He popped the latches and opened the top.

The briefcase was filled with cash—stacks of twenty-dollar bills.

Mom and I both flinched. She let out a whistle. I had never seen so much money in my life.

"How much is it?" my mother asked.

"A hundred thousand dollars," Agent Pluto said, lowering his voice as if anyone else could hear. "If Joseph is able to complete the mission and warn the president about the Pearl Harbor attack in advance, this money will belong to him. It should cover a good part of his college education, I would think. I know that's a concern of yours, Mrs. Stoshack."

I picked up a stack of bills and ran my finger along the edge like it was a flip book. It felt good, and it smelled like money.

"But if my son dies, he won't be going to college," my mother said, "will he, Mr. Pluto?"

"I suppose there is a very slim chance of that happening," he admitted.

"You're a big boy, Joey," my mother said. "I leave it up to you."

I knew one thing for sure. This time I was going to do my homework. After Agent Pluto left, I went to my room and studied the newspaper articles Flip had given me. I leafed through the baseball books on my shelf. I went online and learned a few things I didn't know about Ted Williams.

He was really young in 1941, I discovered. His birthday was August 30, 1918, so during the summer of 1941 he would be turning 23 years old. A baby, practically. He was only in his third year in the majors when he hit .406. He was so sharp that season that he only struck out 27 times. That's about once a week.

Hitting over .400 was a big deal in 1941, and Williams's accomplishment would be even bigger today. I learned that since 1941 the rule was changed so that a sacrifice fly was no longer counted as an at-bat. Ted had a number of sac flies that season, and if he was playing under today's rules, his average would have been even higher: .411.

I went to Google Images and found hundreds of pictures of Ted Williams. I wanted to get a good look at him so I would recognize him as soon as I saw him in 1941.

I also read the article Agent Pluto had given me about Pearl Harbor. The naval station was attacked by 350 Japanese planes that day, and the whole attack lasted just two hours. In the end, 21 ships were sunk or damaged, over 300 of our planes and all 8 battleships were damaged or destroyed. When the USS *Arizona* was hit, more than a thousand men died almost instantly. It was a horrible tragedy, and so many more deaths would follow. And I was the only person in the world who could do anything about it.

I decided I would try again, with the 1941 card.

I would be lying if I didn't admit that getting a briefcase with $100,000 in it was a factor in my decision. I *did* want to go to college someday. And maybe, I thought, there might be a few dollars left over so I could buy myself a decent used car when I'm old enough to drive.

"Mom, I'm ready," I said as I opened my bedroom door.

I took a new pack of baseball cards out of my drawer while I waited for her. I would need them to get back home when I was finished. I also grabbed the newspaper articles that Flip and Agent Pluto had given me, just in case.

My mother and Uncle Wilbur came into my room. Mom was carrying a little brown lunch bag and a portable umbrella.

"Mom!" I protested, but I knew it was no use.

"You're going to get hungry," she said. "They didn't have fast-food joints on every corner back in 1941."

Uncle Wilbur had a pair of corduroy pants with him, which he handed to me.

"Only farmers wore blue jeans back in those days," he told me. "These should fit you."

While I was putting Uncle Wilbur's pants on, he stuck his fingers in a jar of Vaseline and started smearing the stuff on my hair.

"Stop it!" I told him. "Why do I need that goop?"

"In my day," Uncle Wilbur informed me, "we slicked our hair back with this stuff called pomade. We wanted to look like Valentino."

I didn't know who Valentino was, and I didn't care.

"You want to fit in, don't you?" my mother asked.

Finally, they were done fussing with me. My mother stepped back to look me over.

"You look like a real boy from the Depression," she said.

"Gee, thanks," I said. "Now I'm depressed."

"Nervous?" Uncle Wilbur asked.

"A little," I admitted.

"I'd love to go back to 1941 again," he said wistfully. "See my old friends. I sure wish I was in your shoes."

"You can wear 'em while I'm gone," I told him.

My mother hugged me and kissed me good-bye.

"Remember," she said, "if you get into any trouble at all, you come *straight* home. Hear me?"

"Don't worry."

They left and closed the door behind them. I picked up the Ted Williams card that Agent Pluto had given me and thought about 1941. Where would I land? Ted Williams played for the Red Sox, so I figured I would probably show up in Boston. I had never been there before. Maybe I would go to Fenway Park. See the Green Monster.

What would the world be like in 1941, I wondered? Would everybody be running around in those zoot suits I'd seen in old movies? Would they be singing show tunes and dancing around with top hats and canes?

I closed my eyes. A few minutes went by before I started to feel the tingling sensation in my fingertips. I was used to it by now, so I didn't freak out. It felt good. I relaxed. The card was doing its thing. Just another trip to . . . somewhere.

Goose pimples formed on my arms as the tingling spread across my body. I shivered a little as the feeling washed over me. It wouldn't be long now. I felt myself losing weight, almost like I was rising up off the bed. But that wasn't it, I knew. The atoms, or molecules, or *whatever* it was that made up my body were disappearing from the twenty-first century so they could reconstitute themselves in 1941. I wished I could open my eyes to see it happen. But they wouldn't open. They were sealed shut.

It didn't matter. I was already gone.

Where Am I?

I OPENED MY EYES, BUT THERE WASN'T MUCH TO SEE. IT WAS dark out. I was standing on a street corner, and the streetlights were dimmer than I remembered them. There were tall buildings around, and cars parked on both sides of a wide avenue. It was a big city—Boston, I figured. So far, so good. At least I wasn't in another plane.

I looked up to read the street sign. The wide street was called Market, and the smaller cross street was 8th.

It was warm out, but not hot. It felt like the end of the summer when it's just starting to get chilly at night in anticipation of fall. Good. If it was really cold, I would worry because that would mean I might have arrived after December 7—the date Pearl Harbor was attacked.

One of the first things I noticed was the cars on

the street. It wasn't that they were *old*. I knew that cars from the 1940s were big and rounded, and a lot of them had whitewall tires. No, the surprising thing about the cars was that they were *filthy*. Back home there's an antique car show every year, and the cars are always shiny and perfect. So I naturally assumed that cars in the old days looked like that too. But now that I was seeing them with my own eyes, I noticed that a lot of them were dirty and dented. They hadn't been restored.

Not many people were out on the street. *It must be pretty late at night,* I figured. I certainly didn't see Ted Williams anywhere.

But it was okay. That was the way it always worked—I would land in the general vicinity of the player on the card. Then I would have to find him. Time travel is not an exact science.

Maybe I was a few blocks from Fenway Park, I guessed. I used the old eenie, meenie, miney, moe system to pick a direction and started walking down Market Street. I kept turning around as I walked to make sure nobody was following me. More than anything else, I didn't want to get mugged. If somebody took my pack of new baseball cards, I would never be able to get back to my own time. I patted my pocket to make sure I still had it.

The first cross street I came to was 7th Street, so I made a mental note that I was walking downtown. On the corner was a little brick house with a sign in front of it. I had to get up close to it to read the words . . .

Huh! I didn't know the Declaration of Independence had been written in Boston.

After walking a couple of blocks, I was beginning to get discouraged. Maybe I was walking in the wrong direction. What if Ted Williams was *uptown* somewhere? I decided to ask for directions.

A man wearing a hat was walking down the sidewalk toward me.

"Excuse me," I asked him, "which way to Fenway Park?"

The guy gave me a weird look and walked by without responding. He probably thought I was going to hit him up for money.

A man and a woman were coming toward me arm in arm. The guy also was wearing a hat. It occurred to me that *all* the men were wearing hats. I guess men wore hats in those days, even in the summer.

"Am I heading toward Fenway Park?" I asked the couple.

The woman giggled and pulled her man away from me as if I had a contagious disease.

"What are you, a wise guy?" the man said as they hurried past me, laughing.

Maybe this *wasn't* Boston, it occurred to me.

I spotted a garbage can on the next corner and rushed over there. Just as I'd hoped, there was a newspaper in it. I grabbed it.

Philadelphia?

Of *course!* The Declaration of Independence wasn't written in Boston. It was written in Philadelphia. We learned that in school. No wonder those people looked at me strangely when I'd asked them how to get to Fenway Park.

I sat down on a bench between 6th and 5th Streets to think things over. What was I doing in

Philadelphia? Ted Williams played for the Red Sox in the American League. The Phillies were in the National League. I knew that back in the old days, there was no interleague play. The Phillies and Red Sox would never play each other. Something must have gone wrong. Again.

I cursed my bad luck. How come I never land where I *want* to land? The last time, when I went to see Roberto Clemente, I landed in New York even though Clemente was in Cincinnati. Now I had landed in Philly even though Williams was in Boston. Just *once* I wish it was easy.

It looked like I would have to take a train to Boston. I didn't know where the train station was or if the trains ran at night. And I didn't even think to bring money with me. This was not looking good.

I scanned the front page of the newspaper. I always liked newspapers. You can learn a lot of stuff from them. A lot of people, I know, use electronic readers now. But I like the feeling of paper.

A nearby streetlamp was bright enough so I could read. I squinted to see the date at the top of the front page: September 27, 1941.

Well, at least my timing was right. It was about ten weeks before the attack on Pearl Harbor.

The front page was filled with stories about the war raging in Europe. An article said that Nazi U-boats were terrorizing the North Atlantic Ocean. The German air force, the Luftwaffe, was bombing England. Germany's biggest battleship, the

Bismarck, had been sunk on May 27. Hitler invaded the Soviet Union on June 22, and the Nazis had just reached Leningrad.

Nothing about Japan. At least according to the newspaper, Japan wasn't even considered a threat. No wonder the attack on Pearl Harbor came as such a surprise.

I turned to the sports section. The Brooklyn Dodgers had won the National League pennant, and the Yankees had won in the American League. The World Series was scheduled to begin in three days at Yankee Stadium. The second page of the sports section had an article about Ted Williams.

WILLIAMS AT .3996 AS RED SOX WIN, 5-1

Star Batter Slips Below .400 Goal, Hitting One for Four Against Athletics

PHILADELPHIA, Sept. 27 (AP) —Ted Williams, striving to become the first major leaguer in eleven years to bat .400 for a season, made only one hit in four chances today and dropped just below .400 as the Red Sox defeated the Athletics, 5 to 1.

Swinging against a rookie, Roger Wolff, Williams doubled once and was retired thrice, once on a strike out. He walked in his first turn at the plate. That trimmed his average from .4009 to .3996, with only two games left in which to re-enter the select class.

September 28—the next day—would be the last day of baseball season. Ted's batting average stood at .39955—just below the magical .400 mark. It would all come down to a doubleheader the next day against . . . THE PHILADELPHIA ATHLETICS.

That's right! Back in the old days, Philadelphia had a team in the American League called the Athletics, or the A's. The Red Sox were going to play the Philadelphia Athletics on the last day of the season. That meant that Ted Williams was in Philadelphia!

So *that's* why I landed here. I didn't have to take a train to Boston. Ted Williams was somewhere near me. I just had to track him down.

He was probably staying in a hotel nearby, I figured. I stuffed the newspaper back into the garbage can and looked around. There was a grassy field behind me and a grand-looking building at the other end, about a block away. It could be a hotel. Somehow, it looked familiar. I walked toward it.

I remembered the building. We had learned about it in school.

As I got closer to the building, I remembered that I had seen it before. Twice, in fact. It was in my Social Studies textbook and also in that movie *National Treasure*. This wasn't any hotel. It was Independence Hall! Thomas Jefferson wrote the Declaration of Independence a few blocks away from this spot, and then he must have walked down Market Street to this building, where the declaration was signed. I remembered that the United States Constitution was also written in this very same building. I had a test on all this stuff at school just a few weeks earlier.

Finding Ted Williams could wait.

In the twenty-first century, I would bet, you can't get close to an historic building like this one. They probably have barricades all around it, and armed guards. But on this night, in 1941, there was nobody around. I could walk right up to the building and touch it.

I stood on my tiptoes to look inside the window. There were no lights on inside Independence Hall; but from the streetlights and the light of the moon, I could see a faint outline of something that was familiar to me.

It was the Liberty Bell.

There it was. I could even see the crack. I couldn't make out the words written on it, but I knew what they were because we had to memorize them for a test: "Proclaim LIBERTY throughout all the Land unto all the inhabitants thereof."

I stood there for a few minutes marveling at the

fact that I was standing with my nose against the window of the building in which our country was born. I was staring at the symbol of America, and the most famous bell in the world. I was so caught up in the moment that I didn't notice the guy standing next to me.

"It's a beautiful thing, huh?" he said.

I glanced at him. He was a tall guy, maybe 6 feet 3 or so, and thin. He had long legs and a long neck, which made him slightly goofy looking. I recognized the face.

"You're not . . ."

"The name is Williams," he said, sticking out his hand, "Ted Williams."

9

The Heebie-Jeebies

I JUST STARED AT TED WILLIAMS'S FACE FOR THE LONGEST time. He probably thought I was crazy.

It was obviously the same guy I had met the first time, in the plane. He had the same curly black hair and bushy eyebrows. But he was so much younger now. Twelve years, I quickly calculated. In 1941, Ted Williams was just ten years older than me.

The biggest difference was that he was so skinny. I recalled his nicknames: the Splendid Splinter, the Stringbean Slugger, and Toothpick Ted. It didn't look like the man standing next to me was capable of hitting one home run, much less 521 of them. He must have had a perfect swing.

"You look so different," I blurted out.

Ted looked at me oddly.

"Different from what?" he asked. "Did I meet you before?"

"In the plane . . ."

As soon as the words left my mouth, I realized it was a stupid thing to say. For all I knew, Ted Williams hadn't even had his first plane ride yet.

"What plane?" he asked. "Are you nuts, Junior?"

I could have slapped myself. *It's 1941, idiot! When we crash-landed in South Korea, it was 1953. He's not going to know about that. It didn't happen yet.*

"I'm sorry," I said, flustered. "I'm a little nervous. I never met anybody famous before."

"Forget it," he replied. "What are you doing out on the streets this late at night? Are you lost?"

He had that same loud voice but seemed a little more soft-spoken than he would become in 1953. He wasn't cursing as much either.

"No," I said. "I'm just out . . . walking around."

"Do your mom and dad know you're here?" he asked, sounding genuinely concerned.

"Well, yeah," I said. "I mean no. Not exactly."

"Where are they?"

"In Kentucky," I told him. "Louisville."

"Louisville?" Ted asked. "Did you run away from home? You're gonna get yourself killed, Junior! There are all kinds of nuts roaming the streets at this hour, y'know. I'm sending you home. What's your name?"

"No, don't send me home!" I exclaimed. "Look, my name is Joe Stoshack. I'm not lost. I didn't run away from home. I'm fine. It's a long story."

And this wasn't the time to tell it. I knew that if I told Ted Williams I came from the future and that I can travel through time with baseball cards, he would be *sure* I was crazy. He might take me to a mental hospital or something. No, I would have to win his trust before telling him the truth about why I was there. I would wait until the time was right.

Famous people, I'd heard, usually care about one thing more than anything else: themselves. I thought it would be best to change the subject—to Ted.

"What are *you* doing out here so late?" I asked him. "Don't you have a game tomorrow?"

"Two," he replied. "A doubleheader. I like to walk at night. It helps me think. You wanna keep me company for a while, Junior?"

"Sure."

He pulled a shapeless, rumpled hat out of his pocket and put it on.

"I don't want to be recognized by anybody else," he said.

I glanced at a sign on the corner and saw that we were on Chestnut Street. Ted seemed to know where he was heading. I followed. He walked quickly with his head down, as if he was looking for change on the sidewalk.

I noticed for the first time that he had a pink rubber ball in his right hand, and he was squeezing it.

"What's the ball for?" I asked.

"It makes my hands strong," he replied.

We crossed 5th Street. A park was on the right, and there was a homeless man wrapped in a blanket asleep on a park bench. There was a shopping cart next to him with some bags in it. Ted stopped for a moment in front of the guy.

"Look at that," he said disgustedly, "a block from the Liberty Bell. How could a country as rich as America have people living like that? It's a sin."

Ted pulled a bill out of his wallet and slipped it into the homeless man's bag. The guy never woke up.

"You said walking helps you think," I said to Ted as we crossed 4th Street. "So what are you thinking about?"

"I got the heebie-jeebies," Ted said.

"Huh?" I had no idea what that meant. It sounded like a disease.

"You probably know about the whole .400 thing," Ted said.

"Yeah," I said, "your batting average is .399, and tomorrow's the last day of the season."

"It's .3995535, actually," he said. "If I stopped playing right now, it would be rounded up to an even .400. We're not fighting for the pennant or anything. The games tomorrow don't matter. So Cronin said I could sit out the doubleheader if I want to. It would go into the record books as .400."

I remembered the name Joe Cronin. I had read about him in my baseball books. He was a Hall of Famer who became the manager of the Red Sox after his career was over.

"So that's why you have the heebie-jeebies?" I asked. "What's the problem?"

"The problem is, that's not the way The Kid does

things," he replied. "You don't become great by sitting on a bench."

The Kid. That was another one of his nicknames, I remembered, and he used it himself.

I wondered if the athletes of the twenty-first century would feel the same way as Ted. If any of today's players hit .400 for a season, it would be *huge*. The guy would be all over the news. He'd get his picture on a Wheaties box. He would make millions of dollars doing TV commercials. And if he was hitting .3995535 going into the last day of the season, I would bet he would sit out that last game rather than risk dipping below an official .400 batting average. His agent would insist on it. The players in 1941 didn't even have agents. They hardly made any money, anyway.

But as we turned right on 3rd Street around the perimeter of the park, it was obvious that Ted was struggling with his decision about the next day.

"It's gonna be tough," he told me. "Unless I have a great day, I blow it. One of the other guys on the team figured it out for me. If I go 1 for 3, or 2 for 6, my average doesn't get rounded up to .400. I finish up at .399."

Ted went on to tell me everything he would be up against the next day. The game would be at Shibe Park, which was a terrible field for hitters in September. Shadows from the stands made it so the pitcher was in the sun while home plate was in shadow. So the hitter didn't get a good view of the ball. And the pitcher's mound was 20 inches high, one of the highest in baseball.

Furthermore, Ted told me, he was not a fast runner, so he hardly ever got any cheap infield hits. He had to hit the ball *hard* to get it past the infield for every hit and hope he didn't hit it right *at* an infielder.

Finally, he told me that over the last ten days of the season, his average had been dropping almost a point a day. Since September 10th, he had only been averaging .270.

I had to be very careful here, I realized. He had given me a lot of reasons why he should sit out the doubleheader but only one reason why he should play: his pride.

I knew that Ted Williams was going to finish the season with a .406 batting average, and I knew what he was going to do in each at-bat. It was in the history books.

But I remembered what my mother had said: What if I stepped on a twig and changed history for the *worse*? What if I did something, or said something, that made Ted decide *not* to play the last day of the season? It would change everything. He would finish the season batting .3995535. That's still an incredible accomplishment. But it's not an honest .400. And it would be my fault.

I couldn't put myself in Ted Williams's shoes, of course, but I had an idea of what he was going through. There had been nights I would lie in bed with my eyes open trying to decide what I should do or what choice I should make. I remember when my next-door neighbor Miss Young paid me to throw out all the junk in her attic and I'd found a valuable Honus Wagner baseball card in there. I really struggled over whether I should keep the card for myself or give it back to Miss Young.

"What do you think you're gonna do?" I asked Ted as we turned right at the next corner, which was Walnut Street.

"I don't know," he said. "It's been a long season, and I'm tired. Maybe I'll sit it out tomorrow."

Uh-oh. This wasn't good. Maybe I had *already* said something that changed his mind. Maybe I had *already* changed history. I had to do something.

We were walking back uptown now. As we crossed 4th Street, I decided to tell him what I knew: if he played the next day, he would not only hit .400, but he would even *beat* .400. If he thought I was crazy and called the cops, well, that was the chance I had to take.

"Mr. Williams," I finally said. "I really think you should play tomorrow."

"Why, Junior?" he asked.

I took a deep breath.

"You're gonna go 6 for 8 in the doubleheader," I told him. "You're gonna raise your average to .406."

Ted stopped walking.

"You sound pretty confident for a kid," he told me. "How come you're so sure of yourself?"

"I just have a feeling, that's all," I replied.

"Sometimes I feel like I can see the future. It's sort of like a sixth sense."

We crossed 5th Street and then 6th. Ted wasn't talking anymore. He was deep in thought.

The park we had been walking around ended at 6th Street, and we continued walking uptown on Walnut. At 9th Street Ted turned right, and after two short blocks we were on Chestnut Street again. We had made a big circle around the park. Ted turned to me.

"I'll sleep on it," he said simply.

"Okay."

He had stopped in front of a big building with a fancy front entrance. A sign above said BEN FRANKLIN HOTEL.

"Where are you going to sleep tonight, Junior?" Ted asked me.

"I don't know."

"You can bunk with me," he said. "I have a feeling you might be my good-luck charm."

We went inside and rode the elevator up to his room. Ted took a blanket out of the closet and improvised a bed for me on the floor. He put on a pair of pajamas, then got down on the floor and did a bunch of fingertip push-ups. When he stopped, he told me he was trying to make his muscles as big as his teammate Jimmy Foxx's.

I don't remember what happened after that because I fell asleep right away.

* * *

Sometime in the middle of the night I woke up. There was a noise. I looked around and saw Ted sitting in his pajamas at the little desk next to the bed. He was holding a bottle of alcohol.

A lot of ballplayers had problems with booze, I knew. Especially back in the old days. But I had never heard anything about Ted Williams being a drinker. I could hardly believe he would be hitting the bottle before this game, of all games.

"You're drinking *booze*?" I asked, rubbing my eyes.

"Booze?" he said, and then he looked at the bottle and laughed. "I never touch the stuff. I'm not drinkin' this !@#$%! I'm cleanin' my bat with it!"

I sat up and saw that he had a rag in his hand. He poured some of the alcohol on the rag and then wiped his bat with it. He told me he did it every night, because a bat will pick up dirt and moisture during a game, which can add an extra half ounce.

"Besides," he added, "I can't sleep."

After he finished cleaning the bat, he took out a scale and weighed it to make sure it was perfect.

It was hard to imagine what he was going through. To me, 400 was just a number. 400 . . . 406 . . . 399 . . . who cares? When you get down to it, it doesn't really mean anything.

"How important is it for you to hit .400?" I asked him.

"I never wanted anything more," he told me. "All I want out of life is that when I walk down the street folks will say, 'There goes the greatest hitter who ever lived.'"

At some point I fell back asleep to the gentle background music of Ted Williams grinding his teeth in the dark.

10

The Kid

"WAKE UP!"

I woke up.

Ted Williams was screaming at me. For a few seconds, I didn't remember where I was or *when* it was. I thought that maybe I was late for school. But my mom never yelled at me like that. It was like a bomb had gone off.

"What time is it?" I asked, bolting upright from my makeshift bed on the floor.

"Eight thirty!" he shouted. "What, are you gonna waste your life away? Let's go get some grub."

The guy was amazing. He could go from being perfectly nice to a screaming maniac and then back again in an instant. It was as if he could turn it on and off like a light switch.

I pulled on the same shirt I had been wearing the day before and went to the bathroom. There was some toothpaste in there called Pepsodent, which I had never heard of. On the tube were the words "You'll wonder where the yellow went when you brush your teeth with Pepsodent."

I used my finger as a toothbrush. The Pepsodent stuff didn't taste bad. Then Ted and I went to a little coffee shop around the corner from the hotel.

I decided not to ask him whether he was going to play or take the day off and finish the season at .3995535. I was afraid I had already said too much and that I had influenced his decision. But he brought up the subject himself.

"I'm going to go for it," he said quietly as we waited for the waitress to get to our table. "You want to know why?"

"Why?"

"Because if I sat on the bench today," he whispered, "for the rest of my life I would know in my heart that I took the easy way out. And The Kid never takes the easy way out."

The Kid. I had never met anybody before who talked about himself as if he was another person. It was a little strange.

"You're making a good decision," I told him.

"I made another one too," he added as the waitress arrived. "You're coming with me."

We ordered eggs and toast, but I could barely taste them. I couldn't stop thinking about how lucky I was. I was sitting across the table from one of the two greatest baseball players of his age (the other one being Joe DiMaggio), and I was going to be a witness to the greatest day of his career.

I would wait until later to bring up Pearl Harbor, I decided. And hopefully, there would be time after the game to talk him out of enlisting in the military so he wouldn't lose all those years of playing ball. It was all good.

Ted gobbled down his eggs as if he thought somebody would steal them off his plate. He no longer seemed to care about where my parents were or why a thirteen-year-old kid from Louisville was hanging around Philadelphia all by himself. He was focused on the task at hand: to hit .400 for the season. While he ate, I noticed that his fingernails were chewed down to the quick.

Nobody recognized Ted in the coffee shop. Either that or they pretended not to. He paid the bill and we stepped outside. It was a gray day. That could be good for a hitter, I thought—no shadows.

It was Sunday, so there weren't a lot of cars on the street. But when Ted put his hand up in the air, a taxi almost magically appeared.

"Shibe Park," Ted said as we climbed in.

The driver recognized Ted.

"I'm an A's fan," he said, "but today I'm rootin' for you, Mr. Williams. Good luck out there."

"I'm gonna need it," Ted replied.

We drove through the streets of Philadelphia, passing all kinds of stores. I noticed the movies that were playing in the theaters: *Citizen Kane. Abbott and Costello in the Navy. Dumbo. Million Dollar Baby*, starring Ronald Reagan. I laughed to myself when I saw a sign on a movie theater that boasted WE HAVE AIR-CONDITIONING!

In about fifteen minutes, we pulled up to a big building at the corner of Lehigh Avenue and 21st Street. It filled the whole city block, but it didn't look like a ballpark at first. There was a dome at the corner that made it look a little bit like a church. But there was a sign that said SHIBE PARK.

A smaller sign said TODAY: ATHLETICS VS. BOSTON RED SOX.

It looked almost like a church.

Athletics. I always thought that was a dumb name for a team. Of *course* they were athletic. They were professional athletes. That's sort of like naming a basketball team the Philadelphia Tall Guys.

I wasn't sure, but I didn't think that Shibe Park was still around in the twenty-first century. Neither were the Philadelphia Athletics. I recalled reading that they had moved to Kansas City at some point and later to Oakland. Maybe if they changed their name to something other than Athletics, they could stay in one town.

Players need to get to the ballpark hours before game time, of course. There were only a few fans milling around: the hardcore autograph seekers. Even so, six or seven newsboys were on the corner hawking their papers. Each one had a different newspaper. I reminded myself that there was no internet in the 1940s. No CNN. They didn't even have *television* yet. People got their news from the newspaper, so there had to be more of them.

I peered out the window of the taxi. The men all wore hats, of course. The women wore bright red lipstick. General admission was $1.10. You could get a bleacher seat for 50¢.

"Fifty cents!" I exclaimed.

"Highway robbery," Ted said.

He told the taxi driver to pull around to the players' entrance to avoid the fans. But as soon as we stepped out of the cab, Ted was accosted by a guy with a pad and pen.

"Oh, crap," Ted muttered as the guy approached. "I can't stand this cockroach."

"G'morning, Ted," the guy said cheerfully.

"Well, if isn't Dave Egan of *The Boston Record*," Ted sneered. "The Knight of the Keyboard. I see they let you out of your cave."

"You gonna play today, Ted?" Egan asked. "Or take the easy way out and coast to .400?"

"You think I'd give *you* the scoop, Egan?" Ted snapped. "Take a hike! You'll find out soon enough when they post the lineups."

Egan scribbled something in his pad.

"What do you think of the rumors that, after the season is over, the Sox are gonna trade you to the Yankees for DiMaggio?" he asked.

"No comment," Ted said. "But I'd sure love a crack at that dinky little rightfield fence in Yankee Stadium. If I played half my games there, I'd probably hit 80 homers a year."

Egan smiled and scribbled in his pad.

"Ted, how do you respond to critics who say you're selfish?" Egan asked. "They say you don't come through in the clutch. They say you wait for walks, and you're not aggressive enough at the plate."

"I'd give 'em a knuckle sandwich," Ted said. "Did any of those creeps ever hit .400?"

Egan laughed. He seemed to enjoy taunting Ted, and Ted seemed to enjoy giving it right back to him. But he'd had enough. He was anxious to go inside and get ready for the game.

"Hey, who's your little friend?" Egan asked, pointing at me with his pen.

"None of your business," Ted replied. "Look, I've got better things to do than make small talk with *you*, Egan. So scram."

"Good luck today, Ted."

Ted replied by spitting in Egan's direction. Then he pulled open a door that led to a tunnel that led to the visitors' locker room. I asked him if he wanted me to be his batboy or something, and he said I could do whatever I want. Nobody would care. I guess when you hit .400, you can do anything you'd like

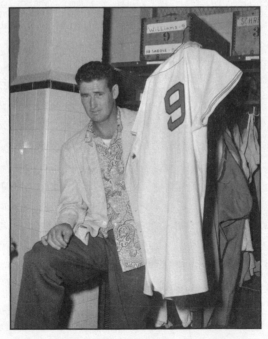

Ted at his locker.

and nobody can do anything about it.

We walked into the locker room, and it was filled with guys playing cards, reading letters, and smoking. In those days, they didn't know that smoking caused cancer.

Ted walked in like he owned the place.

"Hey, Whale Belly!" he shouted to the first guy he saw. "How's it goin'?"

He shook hands all around, calling teammates Sport or Meathead or various combinations of curse words.

"Didn't expect to see *you* here today, Teddy," a player with glasses said. "Thought you'd take the day off and coast."

"I never coast, Dommie," Ted replied. "I go full speed all the way."

That was for sure. If Ted Williams had been around in the twenty-first century, he would probably have been diagnosed with ADD or hyperactivity or something. From the moment he walked into the locker room, he was in constant motion: talking nonstop, clapping guys on the back, cracking jokes. He seemed wired, edgy. I wasn't sure if he was always like that or if he was particularly pumped up and nervous on this day. Finally, he went to put his uniform on.

I looked around, just taking it all in. The players were putting on those old-fashioned, heavy, gray flannel uniforms with buttons down the front. None of them had long hair, a beard, or a mustache. And none of them were African-American or Hispanic. It would be six years, I calculated, before Jackie Robinson would break the color barrier.

The uniforms didn't have the players' names on the backs, but names were written on masking tape above each locker. I noticed Bobby Doerr, who is a Hall of Famer most people don't know about. Jimmy Foxx was another Hall of Fame name I recognized. He was a really big guy, with huge arms. No wonder Ted was doing pushups in the hotel room the night before.

Dom DiMaggio

The guy Ted called Dommie had the word DiMaggio taped above his locker, and I remembered that Joe DiMaggio's brothers Dom and Vince were also major-league players. Dom DiMaggio wore number seven and had black, wavy hair parted in the middle. With those thick glasses, he didn't look like a ballplayer.

Ted pulled on his number nine jersey and hopped up on a table so the trainer could wrap tape around his right ankle. He had told me that he'd chipped a bone back in spring training, so he had to get his ankle taped every day.

I wandered around the locker room trying to pretend I belonged. The batboy, a skinny kid who was chewing gum, didn't seem to mind me being there. He spent most of the time reading comics: *Superman, Tarzan, Mutt & Jeff.*

There was a bulletin board on the wall with the baseball standings tacked up on it. I saw that the Red Sox were in second place at 83-69, 17 games behind the Yankees. The Philadelphia Athletics were far behind in last place with a record of 63-89. They must be pretty bad, I figured.

One of the players stood up on a bench. He had a clipboard in his hand.

"Okay, knock it off, you guys!" he hollered. "Batting practice in five minutes."

Some of the players called the guy Skip, and I realized he was Joe Cronin, the manager. He was the shortstop too. Back in the old days, it wasn't uncommon to have player-managers.

I counted four Hall of Famers on the Red Sox: Williams, Doerr, Foxx, and Cronin. And they *still* hadn't come close to winning the pennant.

The players straggled out of the locker room to take the field. Ted gestured for me to come along, so I took a seat in the corner of the dugout.

Shibe Park was smaller than any ballpark I had seen; it probably had fewer than 30,000 seats. Fans were streaming in, but it didn't look like it would be a sellout, or close to it. Both teams were out of contention. Other than Ted's quest to hit .400, the game was meaningless.

The park had lights on tall poles around the outfield, but I knew that almost all the games in the 1940s were played during the day. Shibe had no padded walls or warning track. If you ran into the wall chasing a long fly, you ran into a *wall*.

The scoreboard was simple. It didn't provide a lot of information other than the inning-by-inning score. There were no video screens, no fireworks displays. The foul pole was just a thin pole. There was no yellow screen to help the umpires decide if a long drive was fair or foul. There were bleachers in straight-away centerfield, which they don't have anymore because it makes it hard for a batter to see the ball leave the pitcher's hand.

I could see laundry hanging on lines in front of some houses beyond the rightfield fence.

The photographers, with those big old cameras, watched Ted warm up.

Down on the field, people cheered when Ted came out of the dugout to warm up. Photographers gathered around him with those big old-time cameras and popping flashbulbs. The other players pretended not to notice, taking their batting and fielding practice. I realized there were no batting helmets and no batting gloves. Their fielding gloves were smaller than the one I have at home. Just about all of the players were chewing tobacco and spitting constantly. The umpire was striding around holding a big chest protector that looked like a giant black pillow.

In the Athletics' dugout, I noticed a tall, thin man

signing a baseball for a little girl. He was dressed in a business suit and looked like he must have been

seventy or eighty years old.

"Who's that old guy?" I asked the batboy, who was the only one in the dugout besides me.

The batboy looked at me like I was crazy.

"Are you new to this country, pal?" he said. "That's Connie Mack."

Connie Mack! Cornelius McGillicuddy! Of course! *Another* Hall of Famer! He had been a player back in the early days of baseball and went on to become the manager and owner of the A's for *fifty* years. I could hardly believe that I, a kid from the twenty-first century, was sitting across the field from a man who had been a player in the nineteenth century.

"All right, boys," the umpire yelled. "Let's play some ball!"

11

I Told You So

THE PLAYERS CLEARED THE FIELD, AND I TRIED TO MAKE
myself look invisible in the dugout. Nobody seemed
to care about me, anyway. If it was okay with Ted for

All the men were wearing hats.

me to sit there, it must have been okay with everybody else.

The fans settled into their seats. Plumes of cigar smoke blanketed the stands—and lots of men with hats. The Athletics took the field, some lady came out to sing the national anthem, and the game was under way.

The pitcher for the A's was Dick Fowler, a tall right-hander. Dom DiMaggio was the leadoff batter for the Red Sox. In the dugout, nobody was talking with Ted. I guess they didn't want to say anything that would jinx his chances of hitting .400.

In the batter's box, DiMaggio tugged at his sleeve between pitches. Ted sat motionless, his eyes locked on the pitcher. After a few pitches, DiMaggio grounded out weakly to short.

Lou Finney, the rightfielder, was up. While he was batting, I realized that everybody—players and fans—were watching the game more intently than people do in the twenty-first century. It took a while for me to figure out why: no instant replay! You had to pay attention to what was happening or you didn't see it. There were no highlights to watch later. No YouTube or DVR. If you missed it, you missed it.

Finney popped up to first base. Two outs. Fowler looked sharp on the mound.

Al Flair, the Red Sox first baseman, was up next. When Ted, batting cleanup, walked out to the on-deck circle, a ripple of excitement rifled through the crowd. Now *everybody* knew he had decided to go for .400.

Ted swung two Louisville Sluggers loosely. The handles were dark because he had rubbed some kind of sticky stuff into them. He dropped one bat and gripped the other so tightly that it made a screeching sound. It was like he couldn't wait to get into the batter's box.

He would have to. Flair struck out. Three up, three down for the Sox in the first inning.

The A's ran back to their dugout, leaving their gloves in the grass on the field. I wondered when that custom ended.

I looked at the lineup sheet on the wall of the dugout. The pitcher batted ninth. There was no designated hitter, of course. That nonsense didn't start until the 1970s.

Ted jogged out to leftfield. As he tossed a ball back and forth with Dom DiMaggio in centerfield, I could tell that Ted was not a great fielder. He wasn't smooth or graceful as he ran and threw. His arms and legs flapped awkwardly. Between throws, he practiced his swing in the outfield. It was clear that the only thing that mattered to him was hitting.

The Red Sox pitcher was Dick Newsome. He looked sharp too, and set the A's down in order. No score after one inning.

"Now batting for the Boston Red Sox," boomed the public address announcer to start the second inning, "Ted . . . Williams."

Even though the Red Sox were the visiting team,

the sparse crowd gave a nice round of applause to Ted. They knew what he was up against.

Before he stepped up to the plate, Ted called me over.

"So, you think you're so smart," he said. "What am I going to do?"

"You mean right now?" I asked.

"No, next Thursday!" Ted said sarcastically. "Of *course* I mean right now!"

"You really want to know?" I asked him.

"Yeah."

"You're gonna hit a single," I told him.

"Serious?"

"Yup."

Ted took a wide stance close to the plate.

Ted chuckled, shook his head, and went out to hit. I checked the defense. The infield was playing Ted *really* deep. I remembered that he told me he was not a fast runner, so he didn't get many infield hits. All his hits had to be clean.

I was watching his every move. You learn by watching the best.

Ted batted lefty. He pounded the dirt off his cleats with his bat and dug a little hole in the back of the batter's box with his left foot. He took his stance close to the plate, legs wide apart, with his bat close to his left shoulder. He let the bat drop across the far corner of the plate to make sure he could reach an outside pitch. Then he wiggled his hips and shoulders a few times, bending his knees as he got comfortable in the batter's box. He pumped his bat back and forth three times, then tapped it against home plate twice. As Ted waited for the first pitch, he twisted his hands in opposite directions on the bat. There was a little smile on his face, and he stuck his tongue out of the corner of his mouth.

Ball one came in, low and outside.

Ted didn't step out of the box between pitches. He didn't fiddle around, pick lint off his uniform, or waste time. He was working. While the pitcher fidgeted on the mound, Ted practiced his swing some more. He looked loose, like he didn't care. He kept his hands low.

Ball two, inside.

Ted refused to bite at anything that was off the

plate. Now he had the advantage. He stared in at the next pitch with greater intensity, if that was possible.

The pitch was away, but Ted liked it. He had long arms, so he could reach the outside corner. He gave the bat a little extra twist before pulling the trigger. His swing was compact and graceful. There was no wasted motion. He threw his body forward, keeping his hands back until the last possible instant. It almost seemed like he took the ball out of the catcher's mitt.

The ball took off like a shot, skipping off the dirt

There was no wasted motion in his swing.

midway between first and second base and into right-field.

The crowd erupted, and so did all the guys in the Red Sox dugout. When Ted reached first base, he turned around and looked at me. I nodded my head and mouthed the words "I told you so."

Dom DiMaggio had a pad and pencil in his hands. He did the math and announced that Ted's batting average was now .401. A *solid* .401—no rounding up necessary.

Joe Cronin signaled for Ted to come back to the dugout and let a pinch runner take his place. Ted shook his head no. He wanted to keep playing.

As it turned out, the Red Sox could not score in the inning. When the third out was made, Ted jogged back to the dugout. Everybody shook his hand, then he sat next to me before taking his position in left-field.

"Okay, you got lucky that time, Junior," he told me. "What do you think I'm gonna do *next* time up?"

I didn't hesitate.

"You're gonna hit a homer."

"For real?"

Ted didn't get another chance to bat until the fifth inning, with the A's leading 2–0. Dick Fowler was still pitching.

This time when Ted stepped up to the plate, the A's tried something different. Their entire defense shifted to the right. The rightfielder went all the way into the corner, and the first baseman stood behind the bag. The centerfielder went to rightfield,

**Ted was a pull hitter, so they stacked
the defense to the right side.**

the third baseman positioned himself behind second base, and the shortstop moved to the right of him. The A's had almost their entire defense positioned on the right side of the field with only one player—the leftfielder—covering the other half.

It made sense, I guess. Ted was a pull hitter. He hit almost every ball to the right side of the diamond, so they might as well stack the defense over there. All he had to do was to poke a grounder to the left side and he'd have an easy double . . . or more.

Ted looked at the shift and laughed.

Ball one, high and outside.

The next pitch was fat, and Ted jumped all over it. Now, I've seen some long shots in my life. Usually, the ball goes up and then curves down, like a rainbow. But this one curved up like a plane taking off. There must have been a tremendous amount of spin on the ball. It was still rising when it sailed over the rightfield fence.

It didn't matter *where* the A's put the defense. They couldn't stop him.

The crowd went crazy. Dom DiMaggio worked it out on paper and told everybody that Ted's average was now .402.

It didn't matter where they put the defense.
They couldn't stop him.

"I told you so," I said after Ted had circled the bases.

"How did you know that?" he whispered.

"Like I told you," I said. "I have a sixth sense."

Some of his teammates tried to get Ted to come

out of the dugout to tip his hat to the fans, who kept screaming for him. But he wouldn't do it.

"I don't tip my hat for nobody," Ted said.

The Red Sox scored three runs in that inning, but the A's put on a big rally and scored *nine* in the bottom of the fifth. The starting pitchers were gone. In the sixth inning, the A's brought in a lefty named Porter Vaughan.

"What am I gonna do *now*, Junior?" Ted whispered to me before going up to hit.

"Single," I said.

The first two pitches were curveballs that missed. 2–0 count. Porter served up another curve, and Ted ripped a bullet up the middle.

".404!" shouted Dom DiMaggio.

"I told you so," I yelled to Ted, on first base.

Cronin sent out a pinch runner to take Ted's place, but Ted waved him back to the dugout.

"No way!" Ted thundered. "I'm staying in."

The score was 11–4 going into the seventh inning, but who was counting? The only thing that mattered at that point was what Ted was doing. The Red Sox got a runner on first, and it was Ted's turn to bat again. He looked at me and raised one eyebrow.

"Another single," I said, simply.

"I'm swinging for the fences," he replied, "just to prove you wrong."

"Suit yourself," I told him.

Vaughan was pitching carefully, and Ted worked

the count to 3 and 2. The next pitch was a perfect curveball on the outside corner, a tough pitch to hit. But Ted slammed it over the first baseman's head— for a single. Ted looked at me from first base. We both laughed.

"I told you so."

".4048!" yelled Dom DiMaggio.

The Sox rallied for six runs in the seventh inning to make it 11–10. The game was a real slugfest. Ted was 4 for 4. He, DiMaggio, and Bobby Doerr had nine hits between them.

"What now, Einstein?" Ted asked me before coming to bat in the ninth inning against a new pitcher named Newman Shirley.

"You're going to hit a grounder up the middle," I told him, "and the second baseman is going to fumble it for an error."

"Get outta here!" Ted said.

Then he went up and hit a ground ball up the middle, which the second baseman fumbled for an error.

"I told you so," I said when Ted got back to the dugout.

"I don't know what you've got, Junior," he said. "But you're sticking with me."

The Red Sox finally pushed across two runs in the ninth to win the game, 12–11. But nobody really cared. The important thing was that Ted had gone 4 for 5. His average was .404, and history had been made.

In the locker room between games, Ted got a

sandwich for each of us, and we sat down to eat them. That's when Joe Cronin came up to him.

"How about sitting out the second game, Ted?" he said. "You got the .400 fair and square. Nobody will fault you if you stop now."

Ted looked at me. I had told him he was going to hit .406. After the first game, he was only hitting .404.

"No thanks, Skip," he said. "I want to keep playing."

I probably don't need to tell you every little detail about the second game of the doubleheader. Ted singled in the first inning. In the fourth, he hit a ball so hard it dented a loudspeaker horn that was hanging over the field. It went for a double.

Even so, the A's were ahead 7–1 in the eighth inning when the umpires decided it was getting too dark to see the ball. Instead of turning on the lights, they ended the game right there.

The 1941 baseball season was over.

Ted had gone 2 for 3 in the second game and 6 for 8 for the day, just as I said he would. His final batting average was officially .406. Or to be more precise, .4057.

You'd think that Ted would have been thrilled with a 6-for-8 day at the plate. But all he could talk about when he came off the field were the two at-bats in which he *didn't* get hits. For Ted, anything less than perfection was failure. That was probably the secret to his success as a hitter.

When it was all over, fans were jumping over the railings and running on the field to get close to Ted. He grabbed his bat so it wouldn't get stolen. The other Sox formed a human wall around him so he could make it to the Red Sox locker room in one piece.

Inside, everybody was congratulating him as if they had just won the World Series.

"They should rename us the Ted Sox!" Dom DiMaggio yelled.

Ted was loving every minute of it. After a while, the photographers and reporters were allowed into the locker room, and of course they swarmed all over Ted. I recognized that reporter Dave Egan from *The Boston Record* who had interviewed Ted before the game.

"How'd you do it, Ted?" Egan asked. "What's your secret?"

"It's simple," he replied. "You just have to know what you're going to do before you do it."

Then he looked at me.

Over the next 70 years, I knew, Babe Ruth's home run records would fall. Lou Gehrig's consecutive game streak would be broken. Humans would go to the moon, invent rock and roll, and create the internet; and the world would change in so many ways.

But nobody would *ever* hit .400 again.

12

The Absolute Truth

BASEBALL SEASON IS *LONG*. THE RED SOX WERE TIRED BUT happy. Maybe they didn't win the pennant, but *one* of them had made history.

After a few minutes of questions, the reporters were shooed out of the locker room. The players could relax, take showers, and get ready to scatter off to Kansas, California, Texas, or wherever they called home. One by one they gathered up their belongings, shook hands all around, and drifted out. Some of them, it appeared, didn't want to say good-bye. Baseball was their life.

The pile of dirty uniforms in the middle of the floor was high. The only player who hadn't peeled his off was Ted.

"There are about a thousand fans outside waiting for you, Mr. Williams," a clubhouse attendant said.

"I'll leave when I'm good and ready," Ted replied.

"Tell 'em to go home."

He was in no hurry to go home himself, wherever home was. Ted leaned back on a bench and stretched out his legs, a satisfied smile on his face. Then he started unwrapping the tape around his ankle. He asked me to grab two quarts of milk out of the refrigerator in the corner, and I did. He handed me one and opened the other, tilting his head back and downing the entire quart in one long chug.

"The guys say I have a drinking problem," he joked after wiping his mouth on a dirty sleeve.

We were alone except for the clubhouse attendant, who was sweeping up. I couldn't stall any longer. Ted could kick me out any minute. I tried to think of the right way to tell him the main reason why I had come so far to see him.

But I didn't have to, because Ted brought up the subject himself.

"I need to ask you a question," he said. "How'd you know what was going to happen out there today?"

My brain froze for a moment. I wasn't sure how to word it.

"I . . ."

The clubhouse attendant left.

"Those weren't just lucky guesses," Ted continued, looking me in the eye. "You *knew* in advance that I was going to get those six hits today. You knew what I was going to do in every at-bat, like you could predict the future. Are you some kind of a fortune-teller?"

"Well, I . . . the thing is . . ."

Ted had no patience for my hesitancy. He picked up a telephone receiver from the wall near his locker. It was one of those old-time phones I had seen in the movies with a rotary dial.

"Okay, that's it. I'm calling the cops," he told me. "You're either a runaway or you're crazy. The police can figure out which."

I didn't know if he was bluffing or not, but I wasn't taking any chances.

"No!" I shouted, grabbing at the phone. But he was much stronger than me.

"They'll take you home," Ted said, pushing me away. "You said you live in Louisville, right? They'll take you to your mom and dad."

"They *can't* take me to my mom and dad," I finally yelled.

"Why not?" he asked. "Are your parents dead?"

"No," I admitted, "they haven't been *born* yet."

Ted looked at me. He put the phone back in its cradle.

"Explain."

"This is gonna sound crazy," I said. "But what I'm about to tell you is the absolute truth. And the truth is that I come from . . . the future."

There. I said it.

"Explain," Ted repeated.

"I don't . . . live in 1941," I said. "I'm just . . . visiting. I live in the twenty-first century. I can travel back in time."

"And how the !@#$%! can you do that, may I ask?"

He was humoring me, I knew. This kind of information was just too unbelievable to comprehend.

"I use a baseball card," I told him. "I hold it in my hand. Then I can travel back to the year on the card. The baseball card is sort of like a plane ticket for me. A plane ticket and a time machine."

"You *gotta* be kidding me," Ted said, waving one hand in the air. "Get outta here!"

I was prepared for him not to believe me. I had learned from past experience.

"Here's the proof."

I pulled the newspaper article that Flip had given me out of my pocket and handed it to Ted.

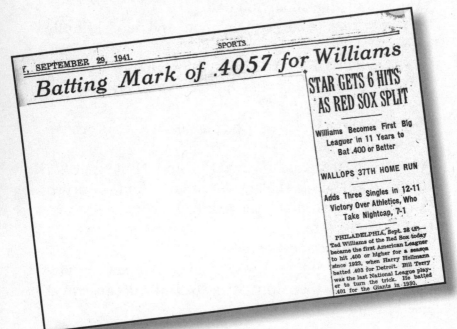

SPORTS

, SEPTEMBER 29, 1941.

Batting Mark of .4057 for Williams

STAR GETS 6 HITS AS RED SOX SPLIT

Williams Becomes First Big Leaguer in 11 Years to Bat .400 or Better

WALLOPS 37TH HOME RUN

Adds Three Singles in 12-11 Victory Over Athletics, Who Take Nightcap, 7-1

PHILADELPHIA, Sept. 28 (P)— Ted Williams of the Red Sox today became the first American Leaguer to hit .400 or higher for a season since 1923, when Harry Heilmann batted .403 for Detroit. Bill Terry was the last National League player to turn the trick. He batted .401 for the Giants in 1930.

"This is *tomorrow's* paper," he said after glancing at the date at the top of the page. "Where did you get it? This paper hasn't been printed yet."

"I told you," I replied. "I live in the next century. In my time, this isn't tomorrow's paper. It's a Xerox of an *old* paper."

"A *what*?"

Oops. They didn't have Xerox in 1941. I corrected myself and told him it was an exact copy of the next day's paper.

Ted skimmed the article and looked up at me. I knew what he was thinking. He had been with me ever since the previous night when we had met at Independence Hall. I couldn't have faked the paper. There was no time.

"Jesus!" he exclaimed. "You're telling me the truth, aren't you? There's no other way to explain how you would know in advance what I was going to do in every at-bat."

"Yeah," I said. "I Googled all that stuff too."

"You *what*?"

"Never mind," I told him. "Look, I swear, I'm telling you the truth."

"Y'know, I *thought* something was strange about you," Ted told me. "Those sneakers you're wearing. Pretty snazzy. I've never seen anything like 'em."

"They're . . . new."

Ted leaned back against the wall again, staring at me and trying to wrap his brain around what I had just told him.

"So people in the future can travel through time," he said, shaking his head.

"No," I replied. "Not all of them. Just me."

"I don't get it," Ted said. "You traveled to a different century just to convince me to play today? If you already knew I was going to hit .406, you didn't need to talk me into it. I would have played and hit .406 no matter *what* you did."

"You're right," I said, lowering my voice in case anyone was still around. "That's not why I came to see you. I'm here for another reason. It's about the war."

Ted looked at me blankly. It was almost like he wasn't sure what war I was talking about.

"I try not to read the papers too much," he said. "It's bad for my eyes."

"Y'know the war that's going on in Europe?" I said. "It's going to become a big deal here too."

"Those Europeans can have their stupid war," Ted said. "It's none of our business. I say, let 'em fight among themselves."

"It's going to spread," I told him. "There's going to be an attack on Pearl Harbor."

"Pearl *what*?"

He had never even *heard* of it. And he wasn't a dumb man. It occurred to me that *most* Americans probably never heard of Pearl Harbor until the day it was attacked.

"It's a big naval base, in Hawaii," I told him. "Japan is going to launch a surprise attack. Here, see for yourself."

I pulled out the other article I had brought along, the one Agent Pluto had given me.

"Japan?" Ted said, surprised. "I thought the war was between the British and the Germans."

"It's going to become a *world* war," I told him. "*Everybody's* going to be involved."

"We already *had* a world war," Ted said as if he still didn't quite believe me. "They said it was the war to end all wars."

"They were wrong," I told him. "There's going to be *another* one."

Ted shook his head with disgust. I knew World War I ended in 1918 and calculated in my head that it was just 23 years earlier—the same year Ted was born.

"This attack on Hawaii," he said, "how did they pull it off?"

"It's going to be a total surprise," I told him. "Sneak attack. They're going to sink a good part of the navy. More than 2,000 American soldiers are going to die in two hours. The United States is going to declare war on Japan the next day, and we'll be in the middle of World War II."

Ted thought about it for a minute.

"Well, if you *really* come from the future," he finally said, "then you must be able to answer this question. Who's gonna win the war?"

I wasn't sure if I should tell him or not. That wasn't part of my mission. I remembered what my mother had said about stepping on a twig in the past and causing a chain reaction disaster. But if I didn't answer Ted's question, he might think I was some kind of a fraud and he wouldn't help me at all.

"We're going to win the war," I revealed. "But a lot of people on both sides are going to die for it. *Millions* of people. We're going to drop an atomic bomb on Japan."

"Atomic bomb?"

"It's a new kind of weapon," I told him. "It can

wipe out a whole city in one blast. It's going to change the world."

"!@#$%!"

"But none of this has to happen," I told him. "That's why I'm here. The FBI sent me to warn the president about Pearl Harbor. If our government knows about the attack in advance, they'll be ready. They could stop it. It would save lives."

"So why are you telling *me*?" Ted asked.

"The FBI gave me your baseball card," I told him. "They thought you would be the best person to help me."

"I'm just a ballplayer," Ted said. "I don't know anything about war."

I took a deep breath.

"That's the *other* reason why I'm here," I told Ted. "I need to warn you about something. You're going to miss four-and-a-half years of baseball."

"Why?" He looked alarmed.

"You'll be in the marines," I said.

"You're out of your mind," Ted said. "Me?"

"After the attack on Pearl Harbor," I told him, "millions of Americans are going to enlist. Regular guys, celebrities, and baseball players too. And because you'll be in the military, you won't be playing ball, of course."

"But I'm just 23!" Ted protested. "This is my time."

"I know," I told him. "You're gonna miss the prime of your career."

There was a look of panic on Ted's face. Baseball

was everything to him. He looked at the date at the top of the article about Pearl Harbor.

"Today is September 28th," he said. "This attack is going to be on December 7th."

"It's ten weeks from now," I told him. "We need to talk to the president."

Ted thought it over for a moment.

"Well, I'm gonna take care of this right *now*," he said.

He picked up the phone off the wall and dialed some numbers. He waited impatiently for a few seconds, and then an operator answered at the other end of the line.

"Get me the White House!" Ted barked.

There was a pause. I could only hear Ted's half of the conversation.

"Yes, the White House in Washington!" Ted shouted. "What *other* White House is there?"

Pause.

"I need to speak to the president!"

Pause.

"I'm Ted !@#$%! Williams, that's who!"

Pause.

"The Ted Williams who just hit .406!" he yelled. "And I need to speak to President Roosevelt, sweetheart. So make the connection. Right *now*!"

Pause. Ted was not a patient man.

"This is a matter of national importance, you little !@#$%!" he hollered. "So get the president on the line or I'm going to !@#$%! your !@#$%! Do you hear me? What's your name? I want to talk to your supervisor!"

Pause. Click. Ted put the phone receiver back in its cradle.

"What did she say?" I asked.

"She said, 'Get lost, creep.'"

It didn't look like this was going to work out. I would have to think of another plan.

But suddenly Ted jumped up from the bench and began gathering the things from his locker. He stuffed them into a suitcase with a sense of purpose. Still in uniform, he picked up the suitcase and headed for the door.

"What are you doing?" I asked him.

"Come with me," he said.

"Why?" I protested. "Where?"

"You and me, Junior," Ted said, "we're going to Washington."

13

On the Road

BY THE TIME TED AND I LEFT SHIBE PARK, IT WAS COM-
pletely dark outside. There were only a few people on
the street. The fans that had been waiting for Ted
were gone.

It was too late to set out for Washington. Ted
said we would get an early start the next morning. I
thanked him over and over again for helping me; but
he brushed it aside, saying he had a friend he wanted
to visit on the way to Washington, anyway. We took a
cab back to the hotel, and Ted said I could order dinner from room service.

Have you ever ordered room service? If not, I
highly recommend it. You can have whatever you
want, and they bring it right to your hotel room! We
both ordered steaks, and a guy rolled the food in on a
big cart. It was cool.

Ted was in a good mood, still on a high from

his historic achievement. And he didn't even know how historic it *was*. Just 11 years earlier, in 1930, Bill Terry of the New York Giants hit .401. People probably thought that every 10 years or so somebody would crack the .400 mark. Little did they know that after Ted did it, more than 70 years would go by with *nobody* reaching that level again.

"WAKE UP!"

I woke up.

"We gotta drive to Washington and tell President Roosevelt about Pearl Harbor!"

It was the next morning, and Ted Williams was screaming at me again. The euphoria of hitting .400 seemed to have worn off. I took a shower, brushed my teeth with that Pepsodent stuff, and got dressed.

Ted was wearing cheap tennis sneakers, a pair of baggy pants, and a red-checked shirt that looked like it was made from the tablecloth of an Italian restaurant. It seemed like a strange way for somebody to dress who hoped to meet with the president of the United States.

"I thought you would put on a tie or something," I said.

"I've found that you don't need to wear a necktie if you can hit," Ted replied.

It was early, not even eight o'clock in the morning. We ordered bacon and eggs from room service and checked out of the hotel. A guy was sent to get Ted's car from the parking lot.

"Hop in," Ted told me as he slipped the guy a bill.

I was expecting that a famous celebrity like Ted Williams would have a limousine or some fancy wheels. But the car in front of me was a Ford station wagon, and it didn't even look new. The inside was kind of messed up, and there was junk all over the backseat. Instead of power windows it had those windows you have to roll down with a crank. And we would need that, because the car didn't have air-conditioning.

Thinking about it, the station wagon was a death trap. There were no seat belts or mirrors on the sides. Air bags? Forget it. They hadn't been invented yet. If we got into a head-on collision, I would go flying through the windshield.

The car didn't even have turn signals! When we pulled away from the hotel, Ted rolled down the window and stuck his hand out to let the cars behind him know which way we were turning.

Washington is less than 150 miles from Philadelphia, Ted told me. I figured that would be a few hours on the highway. We could be in Washington by lunchtime, meet the president, and I would be back in Louisville before dinner.

Only one problem: there *was* no highway. It hadn't been built yet. The only way to get to Washington was to take narrow, two-lane roads. But that didn't seem to bother Ted. He started driving.

Ted's car didn't have a GPS, of course. That

wouldn't be invented for decades. He told me to pull a map out of the glove compartment and be his navigator. I'm pretty good at that stuff, and it didn't take long to figure out that the best way to get south toward Washington would be to take Route 1.

Soon we were out of Philadelphia, and I started to see a series of small red billboards with white letters. They totally baffled me. The first one simply said . . .

DOES YOUR HUSBAND MISBEHAVE?

I didn't think much about it. But then, a little down the road, a second sign appeared. . . .

GRUNT AND GRUMBLE?

Now I was really confused. Then a third sign said . . .

RANT AND RAVE?

The fourth sign really shocked me. It said . . .

SHOOT THE BRUTE

"They're telling women to shoot their husbands!" I exclaimed.

Ted laughed and pointed to one last sign as we approached it. . . .

SOME BURMA-SHAVE

"It's an ad for shaving cream," he told me. "Are you telling me they don't have Burma-Shave ads in Louisville?"

Not in my century they don't. A few miles down the road we passed another series of evenly spaced signs. These read . . .

IF HARMONY
IS WHAT
YOU CRAVE
THEN GET
A TUBA
BURMA-SHAVE

We continued on Route 1 through rural Pennsylvania for a while until I spotted a WELCOME TO MARYLAND sign. About ten miles after that we went over a bridge that crossed the Susquehanna River.

"After we finish talking to President Roosevelt, I'll help you get a train back to Louisville," Ted told me. "I'll drive you to Union Station in Washington."

"Thanks," I said, "but I can get home on my own."

I explained to Ted that I didn't need to take a train. My baseball cards would take me home. It was hard for him to comprehend that, of course, and he drove along without talking for a while as he tried to grasp the idea.

"I'll bet you miss your mom and dad," he finally said.

"Yeah," I told him. "They got divorced a few years ago."

"Mine too," Ted said.

He said his parents were never close and split up when he was playing minor-league ball in Minneapolis. Then he started to talk about his childhood. It hadn't been a happy time for him.

He was named after Teddy Roosevelt, he told me; and he grew up in San Diego with his brother, Danny. Their father ran a little photo studio, and they didn't see much of him. He usually got home late at night, and sometimes he had too much to drink. Ted's father reminded me a little of my father. But Ted said his dad had never seen him play a game in the majors, which was amazing to me. If I ever made it to the big leagues, my dad would be there every day.

Ted gestured with his hands as he talked. Sometimes he would take them off the wheel and steer with his knees so he could express himself.

His mother, he told me, worked for the Salvation Army. That sounded like a good thing, but Ted said he didn't see much of her either because she was always out on the street asking people to donate money.

"My brother and I would be on the front porch past ten o'clock at night waiting for her," Ted told me.

"I'm sorry," I said.

He was talking very calmly now. It was so different from the times he would be yelling and screaming. Today they would probably call Ted Williams bipolar or something and give him pills to keep himself under control.

Ted told me that his mother didn't cook many meals when he was a kid, and she hardly ever cleaned. He was ashamed of his house and didn't bring friends home with him.

"We had mice," he said, and left it at that.

I never saw any mice in my house, but it's no mansion. Money has been a problem ever since my mom and dad split up. I told Ted that we probably wouldn't be able to afford college for me.

"Oh, you *gotta* go to college," he told me. "You don't want to grow up and become a bum like me, do you?"

Despite it all, Ted said his childhood wasn't too bad because the only thing he ever cared about was playing baseball. He would play all day long in the summer. He told me he was really skinny and that he would sometimes eat a quart of ice cream before bed because he wanted to gain weight and get bigger.

"I guess that's why I like underdogs," he said, "because I was one."

We pulled into a gas station to fill up, and Ted casually mentioned that his mother's parents were Mexican.

"You're *Mexican*?" I asked.

I never heard *that* before. He didn't look Mexican.

"Half Mexican, yeah," Ted replied as he got out of the car.

Ted pumped the gas—12 CENTS A GALLON!—and paid the attendant. There was a little market next door. We stopped in to pick up some sandwiches for lunch. While Ted ordered, I walked around to check out the prices: A dozen eggs: 47 cents. A gallon of milk: 54 cents. A jar of Peter Pan peanut butter:

16 cents. A loaf of bread: 9 cents!

At the cash register, the lady asked Ted if he needed cigarettes. I guess just about everybody smoked, so she would ask all the customers. He waved her away.

"That stuff dulls the senses," he said. "Hurts your batting eye."

"It causes cancer too," I told him.

"Haven't heard that," Ted replied. "but it doesn't surprise me."

We got back on Route 1, heading south and west across Maryland. The road was pretty clear, but every so often we would get stuck behind a truck. There was no way to pass. Ted was just about ready to chew the steering wheel off. He had no patience for slowpokes.

A little music might calm him down, I figured. I looked for a CD player on the dashboard until I realized that CDs didn't exist in 1941. For all I knew, they didn't even have vinyl records yet.

The car did have a radio, with big push buttons that I assumed were preset stations. Ted said it was okay to turn it on; and when I did, a crackling voice was heard.

"Must the entire world go to war for 600,000 Jews in Germany, who are neither American, nor French, nor English citizens, but citizens of Germany?" a man asked.

"Who's that?"

"Father Coughlin," Ted told me. "He's a nutcase."

The voice of Father Coughlin shouted again from the radio.

"When we get through with the Jews in America, they'll think the treatment they received in Germany was nothing."

I looked at Ted, but he didn't react. Stuff like that must have been on the radio all the time.

After Father Coughlin was finished with his anti-Semitic rant, a jingle came out of the scratchy speaker. . . .

Pepsi-Cola hits the spot.
Twelve full ounces, that's a lot.
Twice as much for a nickel, too.
Pepsi-Cola is the drink for you.

After the commercial, a song came on. It was big band music, and I recognized the song because last year my mom took a class in swing dancing at a church near where we live. It was "The Boogie Woogie Bugle Boy From Company B." I started singing along, and Ted joined in too. When the song was over, another familiar tune came on: "Beat Me Daddy, Eight to the Bar." After that was a song by a band called Phil Spitalny's All-Girl Orchestra. The music was so different from what my friends and I listen to. Actually, I kind of liked it.

"Oh, this one is the cat's meow," Ted said when the next song came on, turning up the volume on the radio.

I don't know if I can describe this song accurately. It was just about the strangest thing I ever heard. . . . The words sounded something like this. . . .

Down in the meadow in a little bitty pool
Swam three little fishies and a mama fishie too
"Swim" said the mama fishie, "Swim if you can"
And they swam and they swam all over the dam
Boop boop dit-tem dat-tem what-tem Chu!
Boop boop dit-tem dat-tem what-tem Chu!
Boop boop dit-tem dat-tem what-tem Chu!

I'm really glad rock music was invented. I'm telling you, that song was lame.

After that, some other song started playing, and it had equally dumb words. I couldn't make out all of them, but it sounded something like . . .

Hut-Sut Rawlson on the rillerah,
And a brawla, brawla, soo-it.

Whatever *that* means! I can't believe my mom says the music of *my* generation is stupid.

As the radio played, we went though a series of small Maryland towns: Conowingo . . . Peach Bottom . . . Fallston. Then, suddenly, after passing a sign that said BIG GUNPOWDER FALLS RIVER, Ted veered off the main road onto a dirt path. I slid across the seat and slammed against the passenger side door.

"What's the matter?" I asked, a little shaken up. "Is something wrong?"

"No!" Ted replied, a big smile on his face. "Something's *right*. We're going fishing!"

14

If You're Gonna Do
Something, Do It Right

FISHING?

If there was one thing that Ted Williams liked as much as he liked baseball, I found out, it was fishing.

"A guy on the Yankees told me there was great fly-fishing at Big Gunpowder Falls River in Maryland," Ted said as we bumped down the dirt road. "I always wanted to come here."

We drove a couple of miles until we reached the river. Ted pulled over. He looked excited as we got out of the car, like a little kid going to an amusement park for the first time.

He opened the back, and on top of everything else in there was a shotgun.

"You keep a shotgun in your car?" I asked. "Isn't that dangerous?"

"Only to the stuff I shoot," Ted replied.

I have nothing against guns myself. Some of my friends at home like to shoot. But I must have made a face or something.

"Animals die," Ted said as he rooted around in the back of the station wagon, "and nature's more ruthless than bullets. Some folks pay a butcher to do their killing. I'd rather do it myself."

He found what he was looking for: a goofy-looking tan hat, which he put on his head. Then he smeared some grease on his lips and sprayed smelly bug spray all over both of us.

Besides the shotgun, the back was filled with fishing rods, a tackle box, bags of feathers, a bunch of boxes of Quaker Oats, and a telescope. I assumed that he got paid by Quaker Oats to endorse the product. But a *telescope*?

"I like to watch the stars," he explained.

He took out some of the fishing gear, and I followed him down to the water. We seemed to have the whole river to ourselves. There was a little motorboat tied up to a wooden dock. Ted looked both ways and then climbed into the boat as if it was his own.

"Isn't this stealing?" I asked.

"Borrowing," he said. "Get in."

I had done a little fishing with my dad when I was younger, but I'd never tried fly-fishing before. Ted explained that you don't use a lure or a sinker, and you don't use a worm. You use a little "fly," which weighs next to nothing and is made of animal fur, feathers, tinsel, and other stuff to attract fish.

Ted opened his tackle box and showed me a bunch of colorful flies he had made himself. They looked sort of like insects but with hooks sticking out of the bottom. He chose one and expertly tied it to the line. The rod was in two pieces, and he screwed the pieces together. Then he pulled the cord to start the motor, and we headed out on the water. Ted said he had the

We headed out on the river.

feeling that this river was full of trout.

He cruised around for a few minutes until he found a spot he liked. He had only brought one fishing rod out of his car, so I figured this would be a relaxing time for me. I leaned back and put my hands behind my head.

"Get up!" Ted barked. "You don't fish sitting down. Didn't your dad teach you *anything*?"

"Okay! Okay!" I said, jumping to my feet.

"If you're gonna do something, do it right," Ted said, handing me the rod. "I don't care what it is. Hitting a baseball, catching a fish, whatever."

The rod was long, maybe eight feet, and much lighter than my fishing pole back home. But the line was heavier. Ted showed me how to "shake hands" with the rod and to point my thumb at the target.

Because there's no lure or sinker to provide weight, fly-fishing requires a different kind of cast. You have to sort of throw the line itself, and the weight of the line carries the hook. Ted took the rod from me to demonstrate.

"Watch," he said as he brought the rod up over his head. "Backcast . . . and frontcast."

He effortlessly flicked the fly forward, then back over his shoulder, and then forward again. The fly would curl over the line in a smooth arc and settle gently on the water. There was something beautiful about it.

I noticed that he fished right-handed. Ted told me that he also wrote, threw, and did pretty much everything with his right hand. The only thing he did lefty was hit a baseball.

"Here, you try," he said.

I took the rod and tried to do it like he did it. Of course, I failed. The fly flew into the boat, and the hook caught on Ted's shirt. But for a change, he didn't get mad. He just removed the hook and told me to try again.

"Keep a relaxed grip on the rod," he instructed. "Don't break your wrist at all. Use your forearm."

"Like this?"

"There you go," Ted said. "Now you're cooking with gas."

I was starting to get the hang of it. Ted looked across the water, his hands on his hips, while I flicked the line back and forth, perfecting my cast. He was staring at the river with the same intensity he stared at a pitcher about to go into a windup.

"Cast it over there," Ted told me, pointing. "Trout like to face upstream. That's where their food comes from. They like to hang around where the fast and slow water mix."

He maneuvered the boat to change the angle while telling me to bend my knees, check the drag on the line, and cast the fly where he wanted it. He may have had no patience with people, but he had plenty of patience with fish. Fishing seemed to calm him down.

Not me. After five minutes, I was bored and ready to give up. It didn't look like there were any trout out there. We were wasting our time, and I said so.

"I don't like failure," Ted said. *"Ever."*

I kept casting out the fly, but I didn't feel any

nibbles. My arms were getting tired.

"I see one," Ted said suddenly.

"Where?"

"Over there," he said. "See it? See that stitch on the surface of the water? It looks like a zipper."

I didn't see anything. But I remembered reading in one of my baseball books that Ted Williams had incredible eyesight, better than 20–20. Maybe he could see things that normal people couldn't. I handed him the rod, and he took over.

He was staring intently at the water, flicking the line back and forth as he tried to land the fly on a specific spot where he had seen the fish.

"You *know* you want it," Ted said as if the fish could understand English. "Come on. Take it, baby. *Take* it."

And then, suddenly, the line got taut.

"Got 'im!" Ted shouted.

The tip of the rod bent. Ted held the line in one hand to control the tension. Then he pulled in the fly line with his reel hand while he pinched the line with his rod hand. I could see the fish now. It was struggling to escape, darting back and forth.

"He's going left!" Ted said excitedly. "Look at him! Oh, he's a beauty! He's going right now. Watch him, he's gonna jump."

As if on command, the fish exploded out of the water and up in the air. Ted played it, worked it, reeled it in slowly, talking the whole time.

"He's getting a little tired now," he said. "He might

have one good burst of energy left in him. I'm gonna let him run, wear himself out—"

Right after he said that, the most amazing thing happened. The fish came swimming toward us, leaped out of the water, and landed right in the boat!

I freaked out, falling backward and landing on the tackle box. Stuff went flying everywhere. Ted was right. It *was* a beautiful fish. Maybe two feet long. The boat was rocking back and forth, and I was afraid that Ted was going to fall into the river. The fish was probably as freaked out as I was. He didn't know *what* was going on. Ted threw his head back and was laughing like it was the funniest thing he had ever seen.

"Grab him!" he yelled.

"I can't! He's flopping all around!"

"Get the hook out of his mouth!" Ted yelled.

"*You* get the hook out of his mouth!"

I must admit, I always thought it was kind of gross to take a hook out of a fish's mouth. When I used to go fishing with my dad, he always did it for me because I found the whole process to be a little disgusting.

"Here, let *me* do it," Ted said, dipping his hands into the water. "Trout are delicate. If your hands are dry, you might pull off his scales."

The fish had stopped flopping around on the bottom of the boat. Ted picked it up and held it tenderly, like it was a baby. He carefully removed the hook and brought the fish to the side of the boat.

"You're gonna let him go?" I asked.

"He put up a good fight."

Ted lowered the fish into the river, turning it to face upstream, he said, so water could wash through its gills and revive it. He held it there.

"If you let it go too soon," he said, "it won't have the energy to swim. It'll sink to the bottom and suffocate."

After thirty seconds or so, the fish began to wriggle around in Ted's hands.

"He's gonna make it," Ted said. "He's all right."

Ted let the fish go, and we watched it swim away.

He was calm again. Being with Ted was like hanging out with Dr. Jekyll and Mr. Hyde. I thought he was going to switch gears and start yelling at me because of my pathetic fishing skills, but he didn't.

"You're not half bad with a rod and reel," he said. "How are you with a bat? You play ball?"

"Oh, yeah," I told him. "Back home, baseball is the only game I play."

"What do you hit?" Ted asked.

"Around .270."

He spit in the water, a disgusted look on his face. I guess that to a guy who can hit .400, somebody who can't even hit .300 must look really pathetic.

"How many homers?" he asked me.

"I only had a couple," I admitted. "One of them was inside the park."

"Inside the park?" Ted said, looking even more disgusted. "You're a big, strong kid. You should be driving the ball over the wall. What's your problem?"

"I don't know," I told him. "I strike out, ground out a lot."

"Lemme see your batting stance."

"Right here in the boat?" I asked.

"Of *course* right here in the boat!" Ted shouted. "Where else are you going to do it?"

I got into my stance, being careful to put my weight over the middle so I wouldn't tip the boat. Ted looked me up and down, then shook his head sadly and spit into the water again.

"No wonder you hit .270!" he said. "You're dancing around like you got ants in your pants. Who told you to hit like that?"

"My coach," I said.

"Your coach is an idiot," Ted declared. "What position did *he* play?"

"He was a pitcher," I said.

"A *pitcher*?" Ted said the word "pitcher" as if it was something you scraped off the bottom of your shoe. "There's only one thing in this world that's dumber than a pitcher."

"What?" I asked.

"*Two* pitchers!" Ted said. "Pitchers should never be allowed anywhere *near* a bat much less teach kids how to use one."

I considered telling Ted about the designated hitter rule, but I didn't want to push my luck.

"It's about time you learned how to hit a baseball properly, Junior," he told me.

"Right here?" I asked. "In the boat?"

"Of course right here in the boat!" he exclaimed.

I was about to get a personal hitting lesson from the greatest hitter in the world.

15

The Happy Zone

"HITTING A BASEBALL," TED TOLD ME, "IS THE SINGLE MOST difficult thing to do in sports."

We were sitting in the little boat, in a cove where the water was still. The air smelled clean, cleaner than I remembered it in my time. Birds were chirping. It was nice. Ted pulled a couple of packages of crackers out of his pocket and shared them with me.

"Think about it," he said. "For starters, they give you a round ball and a round bat and tell you to hit it square. The difference between a line drive and a pop-up is just a fraction of an inch on the bat. To make things even more difficult, the pitcher could be throwing a fastball, curve, change-up, or some other !@#$%! pitch he's got up his sleeve. He could throw it inside, outside, high, low; or he might just try to *brain* you with it. Then there are nine very athletic guys in the field trying to catch any ball you hit, and they've got big gloves on their hands. Plus, there's thousands of idiots in the stands screaming that you're a bum. That's why the best hitters in the game fail seven out of every ten times they come to bat."

"Or six, in your case," I said.

Ted ignored my compliment. Maybe he didn't like compliments.

"Because you're a good kid, I'm going to tell you everything I know about hitting a baseball. Now, do you know what the Bernoulli principle is?"

"The *what*?"

"How do you expect to hit a curveball if you never heard of the Bernoulli principle?"

Ted told me that Daniel Bernoulli was an eighteenth-century Swiss mathematician who figured out why objects move through air or water the way they do.

"When a ball spins, the flow of air around it becomes turbulent," he explained. "One side of the ball is spinning in the same direction as air rushing by, and the other side of the ball spins against the air flow. This causes a difference of air pressure between the two sides of the ball, and the ball moves in the direction of least resistance."

I had *no* idea what he was talking about.

"You gotta know this stuff!" he hollered.

"Okay, okay!"

I couldn't believe I was getting a physics lesson from Ted Williams. The guy never even went to college.

"There are three keys to hitting," Ted told me.

"The first one is that you need to get a good ball to hit. Now, do you know where your happy zone is?"

"Uh, that's kind of personal," I said.

"No, you idiot!" Ted exploded. "Look, home plate is 17 inches wide. That's seven baseballs. Even a moron like you knows it's easier to hit a pitch that's over the center of the plate than one that's on the corner. The middle of the plate is your happy zone."

"But I can't control where the pitcher is going to throw the ball," I said.

"Sure you can!" Ted said. "That brings me to the second key to hitting: use your head. It's not just about muscles and reflexes. You want to *force* the pitcher to put the ball in your happy zone."

"How do I do that?" I asked.

"By refusing to swing at a bad ball," Ted said. "If you swing at a pitch that's one inch off the plate, the next time you come up, the pitcher will throw it *two* inches off the plate. Then three inches. Pitchers will learn they don't have to throw strikes to you, and you'll never get a good pitch to hit. So if you swing at bad pitches, you make trouble for yourself down the road."

"Okay, I'll only swing at pitches in my happy zone," I said.

"Right. Do you know why home run hitters strike out more than singles hitters?" Ted asked.

"Because they swing harder?" I guessed.

"No! Because they're *stupider*," Ted said. "They go after more bad pitches. That's dumb. Don't chase bad balls. Don't give away strikes. Use your head."

"Okay, got it," I said. "Use my head."

"That also means you need to use the rules of the game," Ted continued. "You've got three strikes and four balls to make the situation into what you want it to be. So if the count is 0 and 2, you're almost sure to get a pitch off the plate. Don't swing at that junk. But if the count is 2 and 0, the pitcher doesn't want to throw ball three, so you're gonna get a fastball close to your happy zone. Bet on it. Know the count. Use the count. Use your head."

At that point, Ted reached into his back pocket and pulled out a little black address book.

"What's that?" I asked. "A list of your girlfriends?"

"No!" Ted yelled at me. "It's a list of every pitcher in the American League. What they throw. When they throw it. Their strengths. Their weaknesses. If you want to be successful at something, you have to know *everything* about it."

Ted told me he would notice the heights of the different pitcher's mounds in various ballparks and write them in his little black book. He studied the wind patterns of every ballpark. He knew which batter's boxes sloped up a little and which ones sloped down. While the other players would sit in the clubhouse playing cards before the game, he would sit by himself in the dugout and study the pitcher warming up. Every day, he pored over the box scores in the newspaper searching for some little tidbit of information that might help him when he came to bat.

"You gotta know this stuff," Ted told me. "Is the wind blowing in or out? Is it a damp day? The ball won't travel as far. And you have to constantly make adjustments. If you ground out a lot, that means you're swinging too early. If you pop up a lot, you're swinging too late. Use your head."

He was throwing so much information at me, and so quickly, it was hard to absorb it. But it all made sense, and I was trying to take in every word.

"Okay," I said, "so the first key to hitting is to get a good ball to hit. The second key is to use my head. What's the third key?"

"The third key is to be quick," Ted said. "Tell me, how heavy is your bat?"

"Thirty-two ounces," I replied. My coach, Flip, had told me that was the right weight for my age and size.

"Are you out of your mind?" Ted sputtered. "I use a 32-ounce bat, and I'm a lot stronger than you are. Look, the pitcher's mound is 60 feet and 6 inches away. If a pitcher throws 90 miles per hour, the ball will reach the plate about a half a second after it leaves his hand. So you have a *fraction* of a second to make up your mind whether or not to swing."

"So you're saying I should switch to a lighter bat?" I asked.

"Of *course!*" Ted exclaimed. "You can swing it quicker. And if you have a quicker swing, you can wait longer before deciding whether or not to commit. And the longer you wait, the less chance you're going to get fooled by the pitch. Bat speed is *everything*."

Ted told me to stand up and show him my batting stance again. When I did, he pushed and pulled at my arms and legs to get them into the proper position.

"Weight balanced," he said. "Knees bent and flexible. Keep your head still. Hold your bat upright, almost perpendicular. It feels lighter that way. Grip the bat firmly. And when you pull the trigger, you want to swing in a slight uppercut."

"My coach told me I'm supposed to swing level," I said.

"I already told you, your coach is a moron," said Ted. "The pitcher's mound is 15 inches higher than home plate. The pitcher releases the ball a foot over his head. And gravity makes the ball go *down*. How are you gonna hit it squarely if you swing level? You have to swing *up* at it."

Everything Flip had taught me, it seemed, was wrong. Flip never pretended to be an expert in hitting. His advice usually boiled down to "See the ball. Hit the ball." But Ted was analytical, even scientific, about hitting a baseball. He was the same way about fishing, and he would become the same way about flying a fighter plane. Probably, it was the same way he was about everything.

"One last thing," he said. "Did you ever hear that joke about how to get to Carnegie Hall?"

"Practice," I said.

"It's the same thing with hitting," Ted told me.

"There are thousands of kids out there who have natural ability. Practice is what separates good players from great ones. There's no substitute for hard work. When I was your age, I practiced until my blisters bled."

My batting lesson was over. Ted yanked the cord to start the motor. My head was spinning from all he had told me: *the Bernoulli principle . . . Get a good pitch to hit. . . . Use your head. . . . Be quick. . . . Use a lighter bat. . . . Swing up at the ball. . . . Practice until your fingers bleed.*

"Let's get out of here," Ted said as we *putt-putt*ed upstream. "We have to get to Washington to tell the president about that Pearl Harbor thing, and I hear he goes to bed early."

16

Visiting a Friend

TED STEERED THE BOAT BACK TO THE DOCK AND TIED IT UP. He tucked a dollar bill into one of the seat cushions to pay for the gas we used. We climbed out and stashed the fishing gear back in his car. Soon we were off the dirt road and back on Route 1 heading south.

There wasn't much to look at for a few miles. Farms and farm stands mostly. We didn't talk much. As I looked out the window, I imagined that in the twenty-first century, this road would probably be jammed with fast-food joints and strip malls. Maybe Route 1 wouldn't even exist anymore. A superhighway might cover this area. It was kind of sad.

After a while, we began to see some houses, businesses, and bigger buildings. From reading the signs along the road, I realized we had reached the city of Baltimore.

"I gotta make a quick stop here," Ted said suddenly,

pulling off the road.

What is it this *time,* I wondered. Was he going to take out his shotgun for some target practice? He seemed to impulsively stop and do something completely different whenever he felt like it. It was getting late. Maybe we'd *never* get to Washington.

Ted pulled into a parking lot. The sign said ST. LUKE'S HOSPITAL. As we got out of the car, he grabbed a baseball from the backseat.

"What are we doing here?" I asked.

"I need to visit a friend," he replied. "It won't take long."

There was no security guard in the lobby. Ted and I walked right in, and he led me down a series of hallways. He was looking for a room number.

"What's wrong with your friend?" I asked.

"Nobody knows," Ted replied. "He's dying."

He stopped outside Room 125 and opened the door a crack.

There were two beds in the room. One was empty, and a boy was lying in the other one. He looked younger than me, probably nine or ten. His eyes were closed, but he opened them when the door squeaked. He brightened when he saw Ted.

"Hey, knucklehead!" Ted said. "What's buzzin', cousin?"

"Nothin'," the boy answered weakly. I could barely hear him.

"This is my pal Stosh," said Ted. "Stosh, this is Howie."

I went to shake hands with the boy, but he could barely raise his arm. I picked his hand up for him and shook it.

"I brought you something, big guy," Ted said, picking up a pen from the little table next to the bed. Then he signed the baseball and put it next to Howie.

"I heard on the radio that you did it," Howie said.

"Did what?"

"Hit .400."

"Oh, yeah," Ted said. ".406. But who's counting? Hey, did they say anything on the radio about the alligator?"

Howie started laughing.

"It bit some kid's leg off!" Ted said, shaking his head. "Awful thing. At the knee. The kid's in terrible shape. Have you seen that alligator around here?"

Howie laughed some more.

"You always say that," he said.

"What's this?" Ted said as he picked up some papers from the table. "Your homework? I see you left some of the answers blank."

"What's the point?" Howie asked.

I knew what he was saying. Homework is a drag. I don't like doing it either; and if I knew that I was going to die soon, I sure wouldn't want to bother spending the time I had left doing homework.

"This stuff makes you smart," Ted told Howie. "You don't want to grow up and become a dummy like me, do ya?"

Howie didn't answer. He didn't need to. They both knew he wasn't going to grow up.

"I'm tired," he said, taking Ted's finger in his little hand.

"Hey, you got a good grip on you," Ted said cheerfully. "How do you expect me to hit .400 next year with a crushed finger?"

Howie laughed. He kept holding Ted's finger. Ted reached into a pocket with his other hand and came out with a ten-dollar bill. He put it on Howie's bed next to the baseball.

"Tell your mom to buy you something nice with this," he said.

Howie closed his eyes, still gripping Ted's finger. Ted told him about the World Series coming up between the Yankees and the Dodgers. He discussed the pitching matchups, and which hitters he thought would come through in a big game. He said he was rooting for the Yankees because they were the American League team, and besides, Dom DiMaggio's brother played for them.

Howie looked like he was asleep, but I wasn't sure. He kept holding on to Ted's finger, and it didn't look like he was planning on letting go anytime soon.

Ted kept talking softly—about baseball, the weather, food, movies he had seen, anything he could think of. Howie didn't respond, but he wouldn't let go of Ted's finger. At some point, I noticed a tear come out of Ted's eye and roll down his face.

Soon after, Ted fell asleep in the chair, with Howie still attached to his finger. It looked as though we would be spending the night there, so I climbed into the other bed and went to sleep.

17

An American Hero

"WAKE UP!"

This time Ted whispered it in my ear.

I was a little freaked out to open my eyes and find myself in a hospital bed. It took a few seconds to remember how I got there. Little Howie was asleep in the bed next to mine. He must have finally let go of Ted's finger. Ted gestured for me to follow him, and we tiptoed out the door.

Back in the car, Ted said it was only about 40 more miles to Washington. We were getting close. I started thinking about what I would say to President Roosevelt. That is, if we could manage to get inside the White House.

"How do you know they'll let us meet the president?" I asked.

"I'm Ted !@#$%! Williams, that's how."

We got back on Route 1 heading south. I wasn't

paying much attention to the scenery passing by because I was too nervous thinking about what might happen to us in Washington. What if we got to the White House, and the security guard wasn't a baseball fan? Maybe he never heard of Ted. Or what if we got inside to see President Roosevelt, and he didn't believe me when I told him what's going to happen at Pearl Harbor? What if he thought I was crazy and had me thrown in jail or something? I just hoped that Ted's fame would overcome those problems. With luck, people would take one look at him and believe what we had to say.

We were driving through flat, endless farm country. Hardly any signs or people. The only stations the radio could pick up were filled with static. It seemed like a good time to talk to Ted about the *other* reason I had come to see him.

"I did some research on you," I told him. "If you play baseball instead of joining the marines, you're likely to get about 500 at-bats each year. In four years, that would come to 2,000 more career at-bats."

"So?" Ted asked.

"Well," I continued, "if you hit one home run in every ten at-bats, you'll hit another 200 homers in your career. As it is, you're going to end up with 521 homers. But adding 200 more would bring the total to 721."

"So?" Ted asked.

"Babe Ruth hit 714 in his career," I told him. "So if you stay out of the military and play ball instead, there's a good chance you'll retire with more homers than Ruth."

Ted thought about that for a moment and then shook his head.

"I don't care about home runs," he said, "and I don't care about beating Ruth either."

"But the other night you told me your dream was to walk down the street and have people call you the greatest hitter who ever lived," I said.

"I don't care about that anymore," Ted replied.

"Why not?"

I was starting to panic. I must have done something, or said something, that changed his mind. Maybe I had messed up history without knowing it. Maybe I stepped on that twig in the forest.

"Hitting a baseball just doesn't seem so important anymore," Ted told me. "If this Pearl Harbor thing is going to happen like you said, all those guys are going to die. I have to stop it. Some things are more important than hitting home runs."

We drove on in silence for a few miles. I was thinking about all those people who were going to die. Ted was probably thinking about them too.

"You and me, we're lucky to be born here," he said out of the blue. "It gave us the chance to be the best in the world at something. If I was born in some other country, I wouldn't have hit .400. I wouldn't be rich and famous. None of this would have happened."

"You mean because they don't play baseball in other countries?" I asked.

Ted looked at me like I was stupid.

"The United States is the only country in the world where it doesn't matter who your parents are or how much money you have," he told me. "A dirt-poor half-Mexican kid like me can grow up to become rich and famous. He can play ball or invent something, start a company or even become president."

"That's what they say."

"Because it's true," Ted told me. "*That's* why this country is great. You know what the most important part of the word 'American' is? The last four letters: I C-A-N."

As I let that sink in, the road took us into a small town with a few churches, a firehouse, and a ball field. There were people gathered on the field, lots of them. At first I thought there might be a game going on; but the people were standing all over the field, and some of them were carrying signs. We were too far away for me to read them.

"What's going on?" I asked.

"That's another reason why our country is great," Ted said. "These folks are protesting something or other. The United States is one of the few places in the world where people have freedom of speech, y'know. If they protested like this in some other country, they'd get locked up. *This* is what America is all about."

We had to slow down to a crawl because there were so many people milling around in the road. I saw a big sign on the outfield fence. . . .

RALLY FOR AMERICA FIRST!

SPEAKING TODAY: CHARLES LINDBERGH

"Lucky Lindy!" Ted said excitedly. "He was my hero growing up. I was eight years old when he made the first solo flight across the Atlantic. He was *everybody's* hero. No wonder all these people are here."

Ted pulled the car off to the side of the road and opened the door.

"Don't you think we should just keep on driving to Washington?" I asked.

"Plenty of time for that," Ted replied. "How often do you get to see a real American hero? Come on!"

As we crossed the street and walked toward the rally, Ted told me something I didn't know about Charles Lindbergh. A few years back his baby, Charles Jr., was kidnapped in the middle of the night right out of his crib. The police found the boy's body a few months later. What a horrible thing to happen to anyone. I felt sorry for him. Lindbergh and his wife were so devastated that they went to live in England for a few years.

The rally was open to the public. I could hear chanting, and now we were close enough to read the signs the people were holding up . . .

KEEP AMERICA OUT OF THE WAR!

LET EUROPE FIGHT ITS OWN BATTLES!

STAY OUT OF FOREIGN WARS!

Some guy handed me a flyer. . . .

I always thought everybody supported that war.

So it was an antiwar rally. I had heard about the antiwar movement during the Vietnam War, but I didn't know they had them before that. I always thought that back in the old days, Americans pretty much agreed on political stuff. Not like today when everybody seems to just argue about everything. Maybe I was wrong.

There was a stage with a podium on it set up near second base, some American flags, and a banner that said DEFEND AMERICA FIRST. Charles Lindbergh wasn't onstage yet, but the crowd was already pumped up. People were clapping, shouting at each other, and passing out buttons and pamphlets.

"Let England and France fight their *own* wars," shouted one guy.

"Let the Nazis wipe out the commies!" yelled somebody else. "Keep us out of it."

As Ted and I moved through the crowd, I didn't have a good feeling. These people weren't peace-loving hippies. They looked angry. I patted my back pocket to make sure I still had my pack of new baseball cards, just in case I needed them.

A pretty woman wearing a NO WAR button stepped in front of Ted.

"Hey there, handsome," she said, smiling, "did anybody ever say you look like Ted Williams, that baseball player?"

"Actually, miss," Ted replied with a smile, "I *am* Ted Williams, that baseball player. And what's your name? I bet it's as pretty as you are."

The girl said her name was Bonnie, and she just about fainted upon realizing that the guy she thought looked like Ted actually *was* Ted. She told him that he was her favorite player and that she had pictures of him all over her room. Ted started singing "My Bonnie Lies Over the Ocean" while Bonnie fussed with her purse until she came up with a pen and a piece of paper.

"Can I have your autograph?" she begged. "Please? Please? Please?"

"I'll make a deal with you," Ted told her. "I'll give you my autograph if you give me your phone number."

"Sure thing, honey!"

Neither of them paid any attention to *me*, of course. Ted and Bonnie flirted with each other while he signed her paper.

As soon as he started writing on it, I heard people around us asking, "Who's that guy?" and "Is he somebody famous?" It didn't take long for people to realize it was Ted Williams. Scraps of paper and pens appeared almost as if by magic and were thrust in Ted's face from all sides. In seconds, he was surrounded by a crush of autograph seekers. It looked like he was almost as popular as Charles Lindbergh.

"It's Ted Williams!" some girl squealed. "The guy who hit .400!"

I wasn't sure what to do. Ted looked up over the heads of his admirers and caught my eye.

"I'll catch up with you later, Stosh," he said.

I wandered around the crowd, trying to get closer to the stage. It would be cool to see the famous Charles Lindbergh close-up. There were more signs up front: FREE SOCIETY OF TEUTONIA and FRIENDS OF NEW GERMANY.

Suddenly, on one side, the crowd broke out into cheers and applause. A man climbed up on the small stage. He was wearing a jacket and tie. As he stepped up to the microphone and a roar went up, I realized he was Charles Lindbergh.

"Lindy! Lindy! Lindy!"

He was a handsome man, and over six feet tall. He looked to be less than forty but seemed confident and sure of himself. I was close enough to see

Charles Lindbergh

that he had a dimple in his chin. Lindbergh waved and waited until the crowd calmed down before he started to speak.

"It is now two years since this latest European war began," he said. "From that day in September 1939 until the present moment, there has been an ever-increasing effort to force the United States into the conflict."

"Boooooooooooooooo!" shouted the crowd.

They weren't booing Lindbergh, I gathered. They were booing because they didn't want the United States to enter the war.

"We, the heirs of European culture, are on the verge of a disastrous war, a war within our own family of nations, a war which will reduce the strength and destroy the treasures of the white race."

"That's right!" somebody yelled.

What? I wasn't sure if I heard him right. Did he say "the white race"? In my time, people who use terms like "the white race" are usually white racists.

It took a minute for it to sink in that I was listening to a racist speech. We had learned about Charles Lindbergh's famous flight in school. But I didn't remember hearing that he was a bigot. Maybe I was absent that day.

"There are three important groups who have been pressing this country toward war," Lindbergh continued, "the Roosevelt administration, the British, and the Jewish."

"Boooooooooooo!"

"Juden schwein!" somebody hollered.

"It is they who represent a small minority of the American people," Lindbergh went on, "but they control much of the machinery of influence and propaganda."

"Down with Franklin D. Rosenfeld!" somebody yelled.

"The New Deal is the Jew Deal!"

Most of the people just stared at Lindbergh in awe. He seemed to have a hypnotic effect on the crowd. After just about every sentence, there was wild applause.

"War is not inevitable for this country," Lindbergh continued. "Whether or not America enters this war is within our control. This tragedy is preventable if only we can build a Western Wall of race and arms to hold back the infiltration of inferior blood."

Another roar went up.

"Inferior blood"? I turned around and saw some people giving Nazi salutes. I couldn't believe what I was witnessing. Even the true haters in my century would *never* insult a minority group or say things like "inferior blood" in public. They would never get away with it.

I looked around to find Ted to see if he felt the same way as Lindbergh. But most of the people were taller than me, and I couldn't find Ted in the crowd. For all I knew, he ran off with that girl Bonnie.

Lindbergh went on for a while saying more hateful things about President Roosevelt, England, and Jewish people. When he finished, the crowd gave him a huge ovation.

As he walked off the stage into a throng of adoring fans, I realized something. If I couldn't find Ted again, my mission would be *over*. I would never get to Washington. Even if I *could* get to Washington without him, I wouldn't be able to get anywhere near the White House.

And it wasn't like I could just call Ted on his cell phone.

Lindbergh had whipped the crowd up into a frenzy. People were crowding around him, trying to shake his hand or simply touch him. Ted *had* to be in that crush of people, I figured. If I could get near

Lindbergh, I could find Ted.

Everybody was pushing and shoving. I tried to make my way toward the stage. What happened over the next couple of minutes was a blur to me.

"Jews control all the money," a guy right next to me shouted. "What's happening to them in Europe is their own fault!"

"You heard what Lindy said," hollered some other guy. "The Jews are leading us into the war to get back the power in countries that banished them!"

Man! Some of these people were full-fledged Nazis!

"What are you talking about?" I said to the guy next to me. "That's ridiculous. If you want to keep America out of the war, stop the attack on Pearl Harbor. It's coming on December 7th."

"Hey, watch where you're stepping, kid!" a boy shouted at me.

"Sorry," I said, "I need to get to Lindbergh."

"Grab him!" yelled somebody else. "He's trying to get to Lindy!"

"He's trying to kidnap Lindy's *other* kids!" a voice yelled.

A giant, burly security guy grabbed my arm roughly.

"You don't look like you're from around here," he told me. "You kinda look like a Jew."

"I'm not Jewish," I explained. "And what if I was? Who cares what I am?"

"He said it!" somebody yelled. "He's a Jew! A dirty Jew!"

"I am not," I sputtered. "I didn't say that. What I said was—"

That's when somebody punched me in the face.

It wasn't the security guy. It was some other guy. I didn't even see the guy who did it. His fist came out of nowhere.

The next thing I knew, I was on the ground. I put my hand to the side of my head. There was blood on it. That's when they started kicking me.

"He's a Jew!"

"Kill the Jew!"

I tried to get up and run away, but they wouldn't let me. One of them had his boot pressed against my head while the others were kicking me in the sides.

I curled myself into a ball to protect myself. *This can't be happening,* I thought. *Not in America. Somebody will stop them.* But nobody did.

Maybe they'll have mercy on me. Maybe Ted will come. Maybe the cops will come. But the only people who came were more Nazis, and their boots.

"Work that Jew over, Johnny!" one of them yelled.

"How do you like it, Jew boy?"

Ted wasn't going to rescue me. I had to get out of there before they killed me. There was only one way. I managed to reach into my pocket for my pack of baseball cards. While the Nazis were still kicking me, I ripped the pack open and took out one of the cards.

"Kill the Jew! Kill the Jew!" they chanted.

I tried to block it out and focus on where I wanted

to go. Home. Louisville. The twenty-first century. Anywhere but here. Fast!

It didn't take too long for the tingling sensation to come. I felt it in my fingertips first, as always, and then it swept up my arm and across my body. While they pummeled me with kicks and punches, I felt myself getting lighter. It was happening. I was fading away.

"Hey! My foot went right through—"

And that was the last thing I heard before I disappeared.

18

Nobody's Perfect

WHEN I CAME FLYING INTO THE LIVING ROOM, MY MOM WAS wearing a leotard, jumping around in front of the TV screen. We got the Nintendo as a Christmas present for *me*, but Mom has pretty much taken it over to do aerobics. She didn't see me coming, and proceeded to kick me in the head.

"Owwww!"

"Joey, are you okay?" she said, rushing to my side when I hit the floor. "You're a mess! Is that blood on your face? Oh, I'm so sorry!"

My ribs were already sore from the beating I got from those Nazis. And now my own mother had kicked me in the head. This was not my day.

"I'm fine, Mom," I moaned. "It's not important. Did Ted make it to Washington? Did he get to meet with the president?"

"What? I don't know what you're talking about."

"Did I stop the attack on Pearl Harbor?" I asked urgently. "Are we going to get that briefcase full of money from the FBI?"

"Uh, I don't know. I didn't hear anything about it on the news."

Of course she didn't. The news is about things that *happen*, not about things that *don't* happen.

I ran upstairs two steps at a time to check the internet. My fingers fumbled on the keyboard because I was in such a hurry. But all I had to do was type "Pea" on Google to find more than eleven *million* websites telling me that Pearl Harbor still happened. All those soldiers still died. World War II went on, just the way it always had. Nothing had changed.

I went over to baseball-reference.com to see if Ted took my advice about not enlisting in the marines. Again, in seconds, I had my answer. It said that Ted didn't play *any* baseball in 1943, 1944, or 1945, when World War II was going on. It said he only played a few games in 1952 and 1953, during the Korean War.

So Ted never made it to Washington to meet with the president. And he must have decided to enlist in the military even though he could have hit a lot more home runs if he played baseball during those years.

Once again I had failed. And I wasn't going to get that money that Agent Pluto had in his briefcase.

Why did this always happen? When I went back to 1932, I didn't see Babe Ruth call his shot. When I went back to 1919, I wasn't able to stop the Black Sox Scandal. I never found out how fast Satchel Paige could throw a fastball. And I wasn't able to save the lives of Ray Chapman or Roberto Clemente.

I was a failure. Only this time I had failed my *country*.

I trudged back downstairs and plopped on the couch. My mom got a wet rag and held it against the side of my head to stop the bleeding.

"Next time, honey," she said. "Next time you'll save the world."

"I don't know if there's gonna be a next time," I told her.

"Oh, I meant to tell you," she said, hopping up off the couch to get something. "A letter came in the mail while you were gone. Do you know anything about this?"

She handed me an envelope that was addressed simply JOE STOSHACK, LOUISVILLE, KENTUCKY. It was a miracle that it got delivered to our house with that address. The letterhead said STATE STREET BANK & TRUST COMPANY in Boston. I took out the sheet of paper. . . .

Dear Mr. Stoshack,
This is to inform you that we have a long-term savings account in your name: #2948283850. This account was opened on 12/8/41 with $1,000 and has remained untouched and unclaimed since that date. With interest that has been compounded twice annually, the total of this account is now $99,875.34. Please inform us

*within 30 days as to what to do with these funds
or this account will be terminated and the funds
will be released to the Internal Revenue Service.
Sincerely,
Kimberly VanderWater,
Long-term Account Manager*

"It's probably one of those scams," my mother said. "I'll throw it away for you."

"No!" I said, gripping the letter tightly as I read it a second time. "It's not a scam. Ted did this!"

"Ted?" my mother said. "Ted Williams?"

"He must have gone to this bank in Boston and opened a savings account in my name," I told her. "See the date? It's the day after Pearl Harbor! The account earned interest for over seventy years!"

"Why would he give you a thousand dollars?" my mother asked. "Didn't you say Coach Valentini told you that Ted Williams was a jerk?"

"He *was* a jerk!" I told her. "But he was nice sometimes too! He taught me how to fly fish, and how to hit. He gave money to a homeless person. He visited a kid in the hospital and held his hand all night. I told him we couldn't afford college, so he must have opened this account in my name. He knew it would grow over the years and be worth a lot of money by the time I was ready for college!"

"A hundred grand!" my mom shouted.

Mom and I started jumping up and down, yelling and screaming our heads off. I was so happy that I forgot all about my sore ribs and the cut on my face. And we were making so much noise that we almost didn't hear the doorbell ring.

I peeked through the blinds. It was Mr. Pluto, that FBI guy.

Mom and I calmed down fast. She hid the letter, and I went to open the door.

"Mrs. Stoshack," Agent Pluto said politely, "Joseph, good to see you."

I knew he came over to find out what went wrong with my mission. I figured I might as well get it over with quickly.

"I . . . blew it," I told him as soon as he stepped inside. "I'm sorry. I never made it to Washington."

"Obviously," he replied. "It's okay, Joseph. I knew the mission wasn't going to be easy. You can tell me all the details in the car."

"In the car?" I asked, apprehensively. "Where are you taking me?"

I figured he was going to take me to FBI head-quarters and brainwash me, or whatever it was that the FBI did to people who failed on their secret missions.

"Relax," he said. "I told you I was a big baseball fan. Well, I bumped into your coach, Mr. Valentini. Did you forget you have a game today? You're late! Get dressed. Get your stuff!"

With all the excitement over playing in the Little League World Series, I had forgotten that we still had a few games left in our schedule against local teams. I threw my uniform on and was still tying my cleats while Agent Pluto drove Mom and me to Dunn Field.

As we skidded to a stop on the gravel behind the backstop, I checked the scoreboard. Bad news. The game was almost over. It was the last inning, and we were losing, 6–4.

"Stosh is here!" shouted Cubby Abrams, our catcher.

"It's about time," said Kyle the Mutant.

I ran over to Flip in the dugout.

"Where the heck were ya?" he asked frantically. "I need ya to pinch-hit. We got nobody left. I used up our bench."

I checked the bases. We had runners on second and third. Two outs.

"Nothing like a little pressure," I said.

"Hey, show up on time and you won't feel the pressure," Flip replied. "Here's yer bat. Get out there and do somethin' with it."

"I don't want that bat, Flip," I told him.

"What?" Flip asked. "This is your bat. I picked it out personally. What's a matter with it?"

"It's too heavy."

"Whaddaya talkin' about, Stosh?" Flip protested. "It's just the right weight for you."

"I'm not using that bat, Flip," I insisted.

"Oh, whatever," he replied. "Just grab a bat and get up there before we forfeit the game."

The umpire was looking in our dugout. I picked a lighter bat out of the rack and took a couple of practice swings with it. It felt good. I could swing it fast.

"Okay," Flip said, putting his hand on my shoulder. "Remember what I taught you. Anything close, take a rip at it."

"I'm not doing that, Flip," I said.

"Whaddaya mean you're not doing that?"

"I'm not swinging unless the ball is in my happy zone."

"Yer *what*?" Flip yelled. "Are you bananas? Get up there and hit! Nice level swing."

"I'm not going to swing level either, Flip."

"What's gotten into you, Stosh?" Flip asked, looking into my eyes. "This is common sense stuff. Level swing. That's the way I teach everybody to hit."

"Look," I told him, "the mound is higher than home plate, and the pitcher releases the ball at least a foot over his head. So the ball is coming *down* at the batter. The best way to make good contact is to swing with an uppercut."

"Who taught you that bull?" Flip asked.

"The greatest hitter in history," I said.

The umpire came over. He didn't look happy when he took off his mask.

"Get your batter up here, Flip, or this game is a forfeit!"

"Fuhgetuhboutit," Flip said to me. "See the ball. Hit the ball. Got a problem with that, Stosh?"

I took a deep breath and walked up to the plate.

"Now batting . . . ," boomed the public-address announcer, ". . . Joe . . . Stoshack."

It wasn't like the Little League World Series, with millions of fans watching on TV. There were probably a few hundred people sitting in the bleachers on the first- and third-base sides. A couple of dogs ran around chasing Frisbees thrown by their owners. There was a baby crying. In the snack bar, they were selling candy and pizza and stuff.

But still, a game is a game. Winning beats losing any day. I like to win.

"Drive me in, Stosh!" shouted Eric Scott, the runner on second.

"You can do it, man!" shouted Josh Cresswell, who was on third.

The wind was blowing out, I noticed. Good. The ball would carry if I could get it up in the air.

I tried to remember everything Ted had told me when we were in the boat. *Get a good ball to hit. Be quick. Weight balanced. Knees bent and flexible. Keep your head still. Hold the bat almost perpendicular.*

I looked up at the pitcher, a lefty. I had never seen him before. Not so good. I decided to lay off the first pitch no matter what so I could see what kind of stuff he had.

He went into his windup and let one go. It was close, but thankfully, the umpire called ball one.

"What was wrong with that, ump?" asked the catcher.

"It was outside," I told him, "by an inch."

Behind me, I heard the ump chuckle.

The pitcher delivered the next one a little high, and I resisted the temptation to swing.

"Ball two," cried the ump. The pitcher threw his hands up in frustration.

"What was wrong with *that* one?" asked the catcher.

"High," I muttered. "Two inches."

Two balls, no strikes. My advantage. I stepped out of the batter's box to think things over.

I thought, *What would Ted do?* I could almost hear him talking to me: *Know the count. Use the count. Use your head.*

If the pitcher doesn't get a strike now, the count would go to 3-0, and he would be in danger of walking me to load the bases. Not only that, but walking me would put the winning run on base. He didn't want that. This time he wouldn't try to hit a corner. He would lay one over the plate. I was likely to get a good pitch to hit. I knew it, and he knew it too. I was ready to pull the trigger.

But I didn't get the chance. The ball slipped out of his hand and bounced in front of the plate. The catcher made a miraculous stop to hold the runners. He got a nice round of applause from the parents in the bleachers. Or at least the ones who weren't talking or texting.

Now the count was three balls, no strikes. He *had* to throw a strike. It was automatic. Nine times out of ten, the pitcher throws it right down the middle with a 3–0 count, and the batter takes it, hoping for ball four.

I looked over at Flip to make sure he was giving me the "take" sign: touching the brim of his cap. But he didn't touch his cap. He rubbed his nose: the "hit" sign. He was giving me the go-ahead to swing away.

I pumped the bat across the plate a couple of times. Eric and Josh edged off the bases. The pitcher went into his windup.

And he put it right in my happy zone.

I uppercutted at that !@#$%! with everything I had.

I knew right away that I'd hit it well. You get that good feeling in your hands. No sting. The ball was up in the air, heading for right center. I couldn't run yet. I had to watch it.

The centerfielder drifted back until he was against the fence. He was looking up.

That's when I saw the ball sail over the fence, take one bounce off the asphalt, and land somewhere in the parking lot.

Three-run home run! We won!

I had never hit a ball so far. A bunch of little kids went running after it, and my teammates went crazy.

They chased me around the bases, pounding me on the back as I rounded first, pummeling me at second, and jumping all over me at third. When I stepped on home plate, the whole pile of them leaped on top of me, pinning me to the ground. If they weren't so happy, I would have thought I was back at the rally being beaten up by Nazis.

As I was making my way back to the dugout, I noticed a girl in the front row of the bleachers holding a little American flag. And I don't know why I did it. I didn't plan it. I didn't think about it. It was just instinct.

I jogged over to the girl and asked her if I could borrow her flag for a minute. She handed it to me, and I waved it over my head to all the spectators. They let out a cheer, and I jogged past the bleachers waving the flag and slapping hands with everybody I could reach. The rest of the team crowded behind me like a parade. We were all slapping hands with the fans.

Somebody in the snack bar must have been watching us. The loudspeaker they usually use to announce that your burger is ready started blaring out "God Bless America."

After me and the guys had high-fived everybody on the first-base side, I led them across the field. I looked behind me and saw that the kids from the *other* team had joined our little parade too. The whole gang of us ran over to the third-base side and slapped hands with the people over there. Then we all ran out to home plate, and a roar went up from the crowd that rang in my ears as they cheered for us.

So what if my mission *was* a failure? I didn't stop the attack on Pearl Harbor. And I didn't help Ted Williams crack 700 home runs. But it was okay, I figured, because everybody makes mistakes. Nobody's perfect. Flip is a great guy, but he's a lousy hitting coach. The FBI agent screwed up and gave me the wrong baseball card. Charles Lindbergh wasn't the perfect hero so many people thought he was. And even Ted Williams—the greatest hitter who ever lived—made an out six times out of every ten times he came to the plate.

I never felt so good in my life.

Facts and Fictions

EVERYTHING IN THIS BOOK IS TRUE, EXCEPT FOR THE STUFF I made up. It's only fair to tell you which is which.

It's true that Ted Williams was one of the greatest hitters ever. The statistics in the book are correct. It's also true that some teams would shift their entire defense to the right side of the diamond to defend against Ted, although that began five years after this story takes place.

It's true that Ted hit .406 in 1941, and nobody has hit .400 since. Anthropologist Stephen Jay Gould called it "the greatest achievement in twentieth-century hitting."

Even so, Ted did *not* win the Most Valuable Player Award that year. Joe DiMaggio did, because of his 56-game hitting streak. By the way, during DiMaggio's streak, his batting average was .408. During that same period of time, Ted hit .412.

It's true that Red Sox manager Joe Cronin offered to let Ted sit out the last day of the season so his average would be rounded up to .400. It's also true that Ted walked the streets of downtown Philadelphia for hours the night before the doubleheader. What's *not* true is that Ted agonized over whether or not he should play. He has been quoted as saying, "I never thought about sitting out. Not once." And "If I couldn't hit .400 all the way, I didn't deserve it."

Shibe Park in Philadelphia was real. It was renamed Connie Mack Stadium in 1953. Two years later, the Philadelphia Athletics moved to Kansas City. The Phillies played in the ballpark until 1970. It was torn down in 1976.

Everything about Ted's military career is true. He enlisted after the 1942 season. While he didn't see action during World War II, he did train other pilots. In Korea, Ted flew 39 bombing missions. On February 16, 1953, his F-9 Panther jet was hit, and he nearly died crash-landing the plane. He was awarded the Air Medal and later the Presidential Medal of Freedom.

It's true that ten weeks after Ted hit .406, Pearl Harbor was attacked. It's also true that before that day many Americans were opposed to the United States getting involved in the war. Antiwar rallies took place all over the country in 1941, and frequently the speaker was Charles Lindbergh.

Lindbergh was famous for being the first to fly solo across the Atlantic Ocean but not quite as famous for being a Nazi sympathizer and anti-Semite. He visited Germany four times and even accepted a medal from the Nazis. The words Lindbergh spoke at the rally in chapter 17 were actual quotes from his speeches.

Father Coughlin (1891–1979) was a real Catholic priest in Michigan who made anti-Semitic radio broadcasts that were heard across the country.

It's true that Ted Williams was a complicated man who could be quite mean one minute and a real sweetheart the next. He would often visit sick children in hospitals, and for forty years he worked tirelessly with the Jimmy Fund, a Boston charity that benefits the Dana-Farber Cancer Institute.

Ted would also give money to old friends in need. He would ask the friend to donate ten dollars to a charity. Then, after he received the check, Ted would anonymously deposit *thousands* of dollars in the friend's bank account. So if Stosh existed in the real world, Ted might very well have put some money in a secret bank account to pay for his college education.

After his baseball career was over, Ted managed the Washington Senators for four years, and he was named American League Manager of the Year in 1969. He was also a spokesman for Sears Roebuck, had a radio show and a syndicated newspaper column, and founded the Ted Williams Baseball Camp in Lakeville, Massachusetts.

It's true that Ted loved fishing almost as much as he loved hitting. In fact, in 2000 he was inducted into the International Game Fishing Association Hall of Fame.

Ted died two years later, at the age of 83. About that, no more needs to be said.

Read More!

I DIDN'T JUST *KNOW* ALL THE FACTS THAT WENT INTO THIS book. I got them from reading other books and newspaper articles, watching videos, and searching the internet. These are some of my best sources. . . .

Berg, A. Scott. *Lindbergh*. New York: G. P. Putnam's Sons, 1998.

Cramer, Richard Ben. *What Do You Think of Ted Williams Now?: A Remembrance*. New York: Simon & Schuster, 2002.

Creamer, Robert W. *Baseball in '41: A Celebration of the "Best Baseball Season Ever"—in the Year America Went to War*. New York: Viking, 1991.

DiMaggio, Dom, with Bill Gilbert. *Real Grass, Real Heroes: Baseball's Historic 1941 Season*. New York: Kensington Publishing, 1990.

Halberstam, David. *The Teammates: A Portrait of a*

Friendship. New York: Hyperion, 2003.

Linn, Ed. *Hitter: The Life and Turmoils of Ted Williams*. New York: Harcourt Brace, 1993.

Montville, Leigh. *Ted Williams: The Biography of an American Hero*. New York: Doubleday, 2004.

Roth, Philip. *The Plot Against America*. New York: Houghton Mifflin, 2004.

Seidel, Michael. *Streak: Joe DiMaggio and the Summer of '41*. New York: McGraw-Hill, 1988.

Underwood, John. *It's Only Me: The Ted Williams We Hardly Knew*. Chicago: Triumph Books, 2005.

Wallace, Max. *The American Axis: Henry Ford, Charles Lindbergh, and the Rise of the Third Reich*. New York: St Martin's Press, 2003.

Williams, Ted, and John Underwood. *The Science of Hitting*. New York: Simon & Schuster, 1970.

———. *My Turn at Bat: The Story of My Life*. New York: Simon & Schuster, 1969.

Permissions

This author would like to acknowledge the following for use of photographs and artwork: National Baseball Hall of Fame Library, Cooperstown, NY, 35, 37, 100. Dan Gutman, 71, 75. Library of Congress, 91, 102, 105, 107, 167. Boston Public Library, 94, 99, 110. Nina Wallace, 109.

Ted Williams— Lifetime Statistics

Year	Team	Games	At Bats	Hits	Doubles	Triples
1939	Boston	149	565	185	44	11
1940	Boston	144	561	193	43	14
1941	Boston	143	456	185	33	3
1942	Boston	150	522	186	34	5
1946	Boston	150	514	176	37	8
1947	Boston	156	528	181	40	9
1948	Boston	137	509	188	44	3
1949	Boston	155	566	194	39	3
1950	Boston	89	334	106	24	1
1951	Boston	148	531	169	28	4
1952	Boston	6	10	4	0	1
1953	Boston	37	91	37	6	0
1954	Boston	117	386	133	23	1
1955	Boston	98	320	114	21	3
1956	Boston	136	400	138	28	2
1957	Boston	132	420	163	28	1
1958	Boston	129	411	135	23	2
1959	Boston	103	272	69	15	0
1960	Boston	113	310	98	15	0
Total		2292	7706	2654	525	71

National League Batting Champion: 1961, 1964, 1965, 1967
National League Most Valuable Player: 1966
World Series Most Valuable Player: 1971
National League Outfield Assist Leader: 1958 (22), 1960 (19), 1961 (27),
1966 (17), 1967 (17)
National League All-Star: 1960-67, 1969-71
Gold Glove: 1961-72

Home Runs	Runs	Runs Batted In	Base on Balls	Strike Outs	Batting Average
31	131	145	107	64	.327
23	134	113	96	54	.344
37	135	120	145	27	.406
36	141	137	145	51	.356
38	142	123	156	44	.342
32	125	114	162	47	.343
25	124	127	126	41	.369
43	150	159	162	48	.343
28	82	97	82	21	.317
30	109	126	144	45	.318
1	2	3	2	2	.400
13	17	34	19	10	.407
29	93	89	136	32	.345
28	77	83	91	24	.356
24	71	82	102	39	.345
38	96	87	119	43	.388
26	81	85	98	49	.328
10	32	43	52	27	.254
29	56	72	75	41	.316
521	1798	1839	2019	709	.344

About the Author

DAN GUTMAN LIVES IN NEW JERSEY. *TED & ME* IS HIS eleventh Baseball Card Adventure (after *Honus, Jackie, Babe, Shoeless Joe, Mickey, Abner, Satch, Jim, Ray,* and *Roberto*). He is also the author of The Genius Files series, *The Kid Who Ran for President, The Homework Machine,* the My Weird School series, and many other books for young readers.

TO FIND OUT MORE ABOUT DAN AND HIS BOOKS, go to www.dangutman.com.

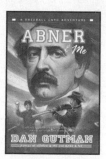